All about the
Golden Retriever

All about the
Golden Retriever

LUCILLE SAWTELL

PELHAM BOOKS

This book is dedicated to my long-
suffering husband, who, for more than
forty years, has been led
'a Dog's Life'.

PELHAM BOOKS LTD

Published by the Pengiun Group
27 Wrights Lane, London W8 5TZ, England
Viking Penguin Inc., 40 West 23rd Street, New York, New York 10010, USA
Penguin Books Australia Ltd, Ringwood, Victoria, Australia
Penguin Books Ltd, 2801 John Street, Markham, Ontario, Canada L3R 1B4
Penguin Books (NZ) Ltd, 182–190 Wairau Road, Auckland 10, New Zealand

Penguin Books Ltd, Registered Offices: Harmondsworth, Middlesex, England

November 1971
Second Impression November 1973
Third Impression November 1974
Second Edition 1978
Third Edition 1980
Reprinted 1984, 1985, 1987

ISBN 0 7207 1217 3 3rd Edition
(0 7207 1028 6 2nd Edition
0 7207 0449 9 1st Edition)

Printed and bound in Great Britain by
Butler & Tanner Ltd, Frome and London

Frontspiece
Sh. Ch. Concord of Yeo

Contents

Illustrations

Photographs

Figures

Photographic Credits

The author's grateful thanks are due to the following whose photographs are reproduced in this book:
H. Bjorkman: 17
Anne Cumbers: 2
F. E. Garwood: 5
Clarence Newton: 10
Dianne Pearce: 1, 2, 3, 9
Barkleigh Shute: 22
Harold C. Tilzey & Son: frontispiece, 4
Lena Widebeck: 13

Acknowledgements

I gratefully acknowledge the help I have received from many sources, particularly Dr Keith C. Barnett, PH.D., D.SC., M.R.C.V.S., who kindly gave me up-to-date information on hereditary eye diseases, and the British Veterinary Association who supplied line drawings and data on hip dysplasia. I am also indebted to the Department of Veterinary Medicine, Bristol University, for authoritative information quoted in my chapter on Ailments. This book is greatly enhanced by the unique drawings on conformation by Miss Marcia Schlehr, U.S.A. and by the illustrations by Mr John Yale.

I should like to express my gratitude to many other friends who have supplied photographs – especially the action pictures of Goldens at home and abroad which illustrate the versatility and usefulness of the breed – also to Mr Christopher Burton of British Columbia who is so closely associated with the origin of the breed in North America, and to my friend Miss Beatrice Jackson, who spent many hours checking the typescript and to whom I owe a debt of gratitude for all her encouragement.

L.M.S.

Introduction

The origin of the breed is to most Golden Retriever lovers now fairly well known, owing to the years spent by Mrs Stonex piecing together all the facts as they revealed themselves. Even so, there still persists the romantic story of the breed's descent from a troupe of Russian circus dogs which for many years was recognised even by the Kennel Club as authentic. Although this story has now been discounted and there is no evidence to support it, there have undoubtedly been dogs of a similar type in Russia. As late as 1919 Lt.-Col.Allesbrook, himself a Golden Retriever enthusiast, recalls shooting over dogs resembling Golden Retrievers in Siberia and Southern Manchuria.

Whatever their origins, Great Britain can claim the credit for the later development of the Golden Retriever as we know it.

It was in the early part of this century that the breed was recognised by the Kennel Club, began to increase in numbers, and between the two world wars it really became established. Its prowess in the field gained it popularity amongst shooting men, and Golden Retrievers could be seen at all Championship shows. However, it was not until after the last war that they became really popular, and their numbers have been steadily increasing until the registrations today make them the fourth most popular breed.

It is not unusual now for as many as thirty to forty Goldens to be entered in one class, whilst at the larger shows such as the Golden Retriever Club Championship Show there may be as many as six hundred entries at the one show. It has often become necessary to have a separate judge for dogs and bitches.

Not only has the breed become popular in this country but it has spread almost all over the world until many countries have their own flourishing Golden Retriever Clubs. I have discussed the countries which I have visited and of which I have a more intimate knowledge in a later chapter.

All the incidents mentioned in this book are to the best of my belief true, and they are drawn as far as possible from my personal experience. I have not attempted to give full statistical information which can be obtained elsewhere, or to name the many breeders of the Golden Retriever in all parts of this country. Up to date information concerning these may be obtained from: The Kennel Club, 1–4 Clarges St, Piccadilly, London W.1.

LUCILLE M. SAWTELL

'The dog in life the firmest friend,
The first to welcome, foremost to defend,
Whose honest heart is still his Master's own,
Who labours, fights, lives, breathes for him alone.'

Byron.

1 Foundation of the Golden Retriever Club

One of the greatest pioneers of the breed was Mrs W. M. Charlesworth who with several others was instrumental in founding the Golden Retriever Club in 1913. Mrs Charlesworth was of Irish descent and spent most of her early life in Yorkshire where she was well known as a brilliant horsewoman and fearless rider to hounds. During World War I she held the rank of Colonel in the Women's Voluntary Corps and in the last war drove an ambulance at the age of seventy. She was for many years the Honorary Secretary of the Golden Retriever Club and in 1932 she wrote her *Book of the Golden Retriever*. It was her pioneering work and tremendous enthusiasm for the breed which established the Golden Retriever as a first rate gundog able to hold its own in the field against all other varieties of Retriever.

Mrs Charlesworth obtained her first Golden Retriever in 1906 and called it Normanby Beauty. This bitch had no pedigree but from her she bred two famous dogs. They were Normanby Balfour (grandsire of Ch. Michael of Moreton and sire of Glory of Fyning) and Ch. Noranby Campfire, the breed's first champion.

Note that Mrs Charlesworth changed the name of her prefix at this time from Normanby to Noranby.

Ch. Noranby Campfire was the grandsire of Ch. Noranby Jeptha, Ch. Flight of Kentford and Ch. Cornelius, the latter being the sire of Noranby Daybreak. From this line many champion bitches were produced in succeeding generations until the post war Challenge Certificate winner Noranby Dumpling who in turn produced Ch. and Field Trial Ch. Noranby Destiny who was later to become the breed's second dual champion in 1950.

At those early Field Trials after the war I was competing with my own dogs and constantly met Mrs Charlesworth both in the field and later back at the hotel headquarters where the evenings were spent discussing every aspect of the Golden Retriever breed. She made a great impression on me and I was anxious to learn from her experience. She had great charm and personality as well as being frankly outspoken with her comments on dogs and owners, and her forthright criticism and dogmatic opinions made enemies as well as many friends.

Her masculine appearance and voice sometimes led to mistaken identity

Teatime with the
children. Owner Mrs
Blaechliger-Gray,
Switzerland.

and I well remember an amusing incident at the first All Aged Field Trial
run by the Northern Golden Retriever Club at Orchard Portman, near
Taunton in 1947. A freak snowstorm took place the night before the trial
and we arrived at the meet to find the ground covered in several inches of
snow. We wondered if the trial could take place in such conditions but Mrs
Charlesworth insisted that 'the show must go on' whatever the weather.
One of the stewards approached her and asked her to move her car from
where she had parked it. I heard him say 'Excuse me, Sir.' She
immediately rounded on him with 'Don't you sir me. Can't you see I am a
woman?' There is also the story of how she was shown by the butler to the
gentlemen's cloakroom when returning to her host's home after a shoot.

She must have been approaching eighty when she was still taking part in
Trials and her dog Noranby Ranter gained a second prize at a Field Trial
when he was twelve. Her bitch Noranby Destiny was handled by Mr G.
Abbott to gain her title and as she was already a bench champion this made
her into a Dual Champion. What a wonderful reward this was after all the
hard work of getting the breed established. Mrs Charlesworth never gave
up. I recall a trial in the north where a dry wall collapsed on top of her.
When those of us around her extricated her from the rubble she remarked
that she had better follow the trials on horseback in future. Her gameness
and vitality were remarkable and no one could have understood and loved
the breed as she did. Praise from her was praise indeed and she implored
breeders to keep the breed active, virile, and workmanlike. It was a grief to
her to see in the ring sloppy, indolent dogs who looked incapable of a day's
hard work, and she took pains to let their owners know it.

In 1950 she retired, to die four years later. I believe that at her death her
two remaining dogs, Dual Ch. Noranby Destiny and Noranby Rally, were
put to sleep.

2 Choosing and Rearing a Golden Retriever Puppy

If you have decided to buy a Golden Retriever, I do hope that you have given your choice every consideration. Have you sufficient room to keep a fairly large dog, and a garden for him to run in? Are you away from home all day at work? Can you afford to feed him as he should be fed?

Golden Retriever puppies are such attractive animals that unfortunately they often go to quite the wrong homes. Their lovely temperament makes them ideal as a children's pet and frequently a young married couple, probably living in a flat, embarks on buying a Golden Retriever without a thought for the life the puppy will lead when they are both at work. Later on when the first baby arrives the new mother is nervous of letting a very bouncy and under-exercised puppy go near the baby.

If he has been purchased during the spring or summer all may be well for a while but what happens when the winter comes and it is dark when his owners leave for work and again when they come home?

Time and again when the young dog has spent a year or more being threatened and shouted at one hears that he 'has to be got rid of'.

By which time the dog has learnt bad habits and is often too old to be trained for work or too out of hand to do much with at all. So he gets passed from home to home on a downhill path.

If you can satisfy your conscience that you can do justice to keeping a Golden Retriever and all the demands he will make on you, then go ahead and buy a puppy and you will have in all probability twelve to fourteen years of devotion from one who thinks the world of you and is never happier than when he is with you. If properly trained he will do your slightest command and take a delight in doing so.

It is worth taking some time and trouble over the selection of your puppy. Although you may not be looking for a top quality dog to show later on it is worth enquiring at a breeding kennel, for while not all puppies in a litter have show potential, they are probably strong and healthy having been well reared. If a breeder has none available he will probably know where puppies are to be obtained because he knows where litters have been sired by his own stud dogs.

Choosing a puppy of show quality, especially a young one, is always difficult, and takes a lot of experience.

If you are a complete novice I suggest that you take someone knowledgeable with you to help you, even if he or she is more interested in another breed. They will know the basic things to look for which are a must in any breed. First impressions are important. The mother should – whether you require a puppy for show purposes or a pet – be friendly and proud to show you her family. Knowing the parents and their background is a great help as you know what faults are likely to crop up and where the puppies are most likely to excel.

Litters vary so much. Assuming that the litter has been well reared and is an even one, at first glance, at any rate to the novice, the puppies will all look the same.

First of all I like to see the puppies running around naturally, behind wire if possible. If you are interested in buying a bitch, ask the owner to shut up all the dogs so that you have fewer to concentrate on. It is quite hopeless to have them all running around under your feet, as you cannot then discriminate between them.

The puppies will naturally come up to the wire and generally sit on their haunches. This is a good opportunity to notice whether their fore legs are straight and the shoulder placement correct. If the puppies are about six weeks old, ask the owner for a table to stand them on and go over each individual puppy. Stand it on the table as if showing it and you will be able to get a good idea of its general outline, length of back and neck. Pass your hands across its back, gently pressing down on its hind-quarters. The more resistance one feels the better and stronger the hind-quarters will be. Weak hind-quarters will give way and the puppy will probably be cow-hocked.

Avoid the throaty puppy which is also likely to be short of neck and upright in shoulder. See that the eye rims are not slack and that it does not show the haw. It is not possible at this age to tell the colour of the eye but if the parents and forebears have good dark or brown eyes it is unlikely that you will have anything to worry about. The eyes do not change from the deep blue they have as babies until they are about twelve weeks old.

The mouth of course must be looked at to see if the jaw is formed correctly. Puppies often resent this but by passing the forefinger between the lips it is possible to feel the position of the baby teeth. If in any doubt make a closer examination.

The top teeth should be slightly over the bottom ones at this age.

Before making a final decision ask the breeder to hold two puppies at a time facing you so that you can compare their heads. Often at this age they have a small streak of white hairs across the skull. Generally speaking this disappears as the puppy gets older but it does depend on the colour of the puppy. If the puppy is dark and the white is very apparent it is less likely to go, but if it is a thin line, then it will probably disappear altogether.

If there is any white on the muzzle I would discard the puppy and sell it as a pet. The white may go but I would not regard it as a good breeding proposition. Try also to avoid picking a puppy if it has white on its feet. This also is likely to fade as it gets older but it does denote a lack of pigmentation. A black nose, black eye rims, black pads and nails are what I look for.

Choose a bold puppy who will come to you and not run away when strangers appear. Do not be too disturbed if his tail seems a little gay – at this age they are apt to carry them a little high especially when they are feeding.

It is difficult to assess the ultimate colour of the puppy, but the best guide is to examine the colour of the ears closely. I think it is impossible to tell whether the coat will be straight or wavy. I have been fooled many times by a puppy having an extra fluffy coat, thinking that it would be wavy; it has proved quite straight when the puppy has grown up! Sometimes one can, however, detect a slight wave on the longer hair of the ear. This is a matter of taste, as both straight and wavy coats are correct.

Enquire if the puppy has been wormed. Some people worm at six weeks, others earlier. Puppies should be done again ten days after the first worming. I worm them again at twelve weeks old. But if you are not satisfied, do the job again as it is better to be quite sure. Worms can cause a lot of trouble later on, particularly when the puppy is teething.

Before you take the puppy home, ask for a diet sheet as well as the pedigree and registration card if he has already been registered. Also ask for a signed transfer form so that the puppy can be officially made over to you at the Kennel Club – you cannot enter a puppy for a show until this has been done nor can you breed from a bitch in your own name unless it has been transferred.

If the puppy is to live indoors decide where his bed is to be, and teach him to go to it. It is important that he should have a place of his own to which he can retreat when he is tired or take his bones and play things.

I am very much against puppies being reared in kennels on their own. It is a very lonely life for them so if possible buy two puppies so that they can be company for each other. It is not difficult to find someone who will buy the one you do not wish to keep later on when you have reared it and your show puppy is big enough to join the rest of your kennel.

Feeding

Feeding methods vary considerably, so one must not be too dogmatic about them but, however you decide to feed your puppy, stick to a regular diet and regular feeding times. I prefer the orthodox method of meat, biscuit meal, milk and eggs.

A puppy at six weeks old should weigh from nine to ten pounds. I weigh mine at this age which is the age at which I generally worm them for the first time. I never let the puppy leave the kennel before it has been wormed for the second time which is at about eight weeks old. (See worming). The diet for a puppy of eight weeks old would be as follows:

9 a.m. One quarter of a pound of meat either raw or cooked, mixed with sufficient fine biscuit meal which it will clear up readily. Increase the amount of biscuit meal as required. This should be soaked in gravy or stock of some kind such as Oxo or Marmite. The mixture should be allowed to stand for about fifteen minutes before serving to the puppy and it should not be sloppy or sticky. Do not use boiling liquid as this is apt to make it sticky. A nice crumbly consistency is best. Add to this crushed vitamin tablets. At this age puppies are too young to swallow tablets whole voluntarily but will do so quite happily when a little older. I also recommend an extra calcium preparation such as 'Stress' to be added to the food. If you are using raw meat it should be either minced or cut up very finely.

This meal should be repeated again at *6 p.m.* At *2 p.m.* and again *last thing* at *night*, give the puppy half a pint of milk or milk powder to which Farex, Farlene or similar baby cereal has been added to make a creamy consistency. I always add one raw egg to every pint of milk I mix, so that each puppy has an egg every day. At eight weeks old the puppy will begin to take an interest in chewing hard biscuits so I give a few after the midday milk. Also give big bones to chew and play with. These are better raw and should not be sharp or splintery. No poultry, game or rabbit bones should ever be given. The amount of meat should gradually be increased so that at twelve weeks old the puppy is having six ounces in the morning and six in the evening. He should be sufficiently well grown now to go on to three meals a day. Leave off the milk last thing at night and give him a few hard biscuits instead when he goes to bed. If you are house training him you will find that this will enable him to be drier at night.

Continue this diet until the puppy is six months old when he will probably not require such a big morning feed. Discontinue the meat and biscuit in the morning and give the egg and milk instead. Increase the amount of milk and give a piece of baked bread or hard biscuit afterwards. The evening meal will now consist of one pound of meat and as much biscuit meal as he will readily clear up. An average amount would be half a pound of biscuit but condition and appetite must be considered and regulated accordingly.

At nine months old the puppy should be well bodied-up and no longer require the milk in the morning. Some puppies, however, are slower developing and it would be advisable to continue giving this milk as long as you consider it necessary. At this age, and to all adults,

I give hard biscuits all round after morning exercise.

House Training

When you are training your puppy to be clean in the house do not expect too much from him at first. After every meal always put him out of doors or take him to a particular spot where you want him to be clean. Get him into the habit of going to the same place. If given the opportunity the puppy will much prefer to be clean out of doors rather than soil the floor.

As soon as he wakes from a sleep he should again be put outside for a few minutes. If this routine is carried out you will have very little trouble at all, but you must not expect your puppy to go through the night without making a puddle whilst he is still having his milk drink last thing at night. If he sleeps in the house a piece of newspaper put down near the door will encourage him to visit it and avoid accidents elsewhere. The old fashioned method of 'rubbing a puppy's nose in it' when he has made a mess is totally wrong and quite unnecessary. A little time and patience is all that is needed.

Inoculation

Consult your veterinary surgeon with regard to inoculation. Twelve weeks of age is the usual time to have the first injection but it does depend on the make of vaccine used.

Distemper, hard pad, contagious hepatitis, and leptospirosis are the four diseases chiefly concerned, and are the scourge of the canine world. In order to obtain lifelong protection, an annual booster injection is advisable but this does depend on whether one's dog is likely to come in contact with possible sources of infection, such as going to shows. A small percentage of dogs do not respond adequately to vaccination but on the whole it is very successful and the only safeguard.

Preparatory Training for the Show Ring and General Behaviour

From the time the puppy is six weeks old get him used to standing on a table whilst you groom him and stand him as if at a show. He will soon learn to be handled and by doing this almost daily he will stand quite still and you will get a perfect picture of your future show prospect.

When he is about three months old he will be too big to lift on to a table so you must continue to practise on the ground. As he gets a little older buy a light weight cord lead and, after grooming, put it on him and encourage him to run up and down. Treat it as a game and he will soon get the idea of following you. In the same way as one teaches a child good deportment, so a dog can be taught to stand and move correctly.

By the time he is old enough to go to a show you will probably be able to hold his interest with a discreet titbit now and again or the promise of something exciting in your pocket. Each dog has to be treated differently as some are over-awed by the occasion and will take no interest at all in food at a show. Others react very well and really look their best when looking keen and interested in what you have concealed in your hand or pocket.

When your doggy friends call to see you, take the opportunity of asking them to go over the puppy as if judging him. This is excellent practice for you both and by the time he is old enough to go to a show you will enter the ring full of confidence in the knowledge that your puppy knows what is required of him.

So often one sees good puppies unplaced at shows because the handler has not done any previous training and makes no effort himself to show the dog off to best advantage. A good and experienced handler will often be successful with a mediocre dog because he has been standing the dog well just at the right time and showing off his best qualities. It is impossible for a judge to place a dog no matter how good he is, if every time he goes near the animal it sits down or lunges all over the place when asked to move.

Quite apart from showing your puppy you must try to make him obedient and domesticated, so that whether at home or out of doors you can rely on him behaving himself. The most useful of all commands are 'sit', 'heel', and 'kennel' or 'bed', as the case may be.

Generally speaking, a Golden in the house takes up less room than a small breed such as a terrier, spaniel or poodle who are constantly dashing about getting under your feet and jumping on all the furniture. A well behaved Golden, on the other hand, will go to its bed or lie down under a table or wherever it is told to go. Nothing is worse than to visit a house where one is immediately molested by dogs with large muddy paws, or those who dribble all over your lap whenever there is food about. A dog should know where his bed is so that he can be sent there, not only when he has done wrong but, for instance, when he has come in from a walk and has wet feet, or when he has a bone to chew. Never allow this on the carpet! Such habits can be taught from an early age. It is not wise to leave a young puppy on his own for too long as he will get bored and start chewing up the carpets, shoes, books and papers, or the leads and flexes of electrical equipment which should always be switched off when he is left to himself, even briefly. On the other hand he should not expect to go everywhere his owners go and must be left at home sometimes. I know of some people who make themselves slaves to their dog so that they cannot go anywhere without him, or even go on holiday because they cannot leave their dog. A spoilt dog is like a spoilt child. A puppy will cry if he cannot go with his master but if he has learnt from an early age to be left alone for a short period, and that you will come back, he will settle down quietly in his bed and sleep. Naturally he will be pleased to see you when you return. Make a fuss of him but do not let him jump up. If he does so, tap him on the nose with a rolled up newspaper. Dogs learn quickly by the tone of your voice whether you are pleased or not.

Teach him to sit by pressing on his hind quarters and saying 'Sit' to him, showing the flat of your hand so that in time he will sit as soon as he sees you raise your hand. Dogs who pull on the lead are a nuisance and very tiring for the person who holds them. I find that the first thing the owner of a new puppy does if not previously advised, is to go and buy a heavy collar and a short lead, often with a bit of chain at the end, and the next time you see them, when the dog is almost fully grown, he will be pulling the owner's arm almost from its socket. I have never yet seen a dog walk without pulling on one of these dreadful leads. Some people seem to think that the shorter the lead the more control they have over the dog which is quite the wrong method to adopt. If he had been trained properly from the start this would not be necessary. A simple cord lead which usually has a piece of rubber around the neck is all that is necessary to start with and as he gets older a lightweight choke chain with lead attached is excellent, but see that it is put on correctly with the running noose at the top.

Some people do not look on choke chains with favour but I am sure that they are the safest form of lead to have as the dog cannot easily pull out of it whilst they can pull their heads through a collar. Never buy a heavy chain. I have seen dogs with chains on them more suitable for leading a bull. If the puppy attempts to pull you can jerk the chain and scold him and he will soon learn to walk properly.

If your dog must wear a collar and if he is not a kennel dog he will have to do so, I recommend a rolled leather one rather than a flat one. Rolled ones are softer and do not wear away the hair around the neck. Remember to buy a licence for the puppy when he is six months old and get your name and address engraved either on the collar, or on a disc attached to it.

Some people prefer to attach an engraved disc to the choke chain and leave it on all the time. This does, however, definitely cut the hair around the neck and if you are showing your dog it will not look very nice. There are a number of attractive show leads which can be bought for this purpose or you can show your dog on a choke chain and lead. It is a matter of opinion but above all do not take your dog into the ring with a collar on him. He must be able to show off his neck and shoulders and a collar detracts and tends to make the dog look shorter in neck than he really is.

In order to get your puppy used to crowds it is a good plan to take him shopping. To start with take an older dog with you if you have one and walk the streets. Choose the quieter ones at first where there is not too much traffic and then gradually take him out in more congested areas always on a lead of course. No matter how well trained a dog may be he should never be allowed off the lead on the public highway. Incidents so unexpected may occur and tragedy strike. Nothing will ever remove the stark horror of seeing a much loved and valued animal either killed or ruined for life.

There are many training classes held these days for obedience and ringcraft. If you are fortunate enough to be able to get to any of these they are of immense value from every respect.

Car Travel

Most dogs love to travel by car, and it is a very good idea to start taking them out as soon as possible for short runs. If you can arrange for a passenger to nurse the puppy whilst it is very small it will gain confidence and very soon look forward to an outing of this kind. By the time it is old enough to sit at the back of the car and not need nursing, it will be so hpapy to be going out with you that it will not think about being sick. It is usually older puppies who have never been introduced to a car that take a dislike to this form of travelling, especially if they are put on the back seat of a car to be thrown from side to side with no one to support them.

Shooting brakes and estate cars are by far the best mode of transport, especially if you intend going to many shows. The surface is flat and the dogs are able to lie down comfortably without being thrown about. It is sitting up and swaying about which brings on sickness. The bottom of the estate car should have a carpet or rug placed on it. I find that Duralay cut to the shape of the floor is excellent as it provides a nice resilient surface without being too springy. A travelling rug placed on top of this makes it very comfortable and can easily be taken out for washing.

Some dogs dribble badly in a car and they are almost as much of a nuisance as a dog who is sick. This can, however, be overcome by giving it a Chloretone capsule which is obtainable from your veterinary surgeon.

This should be given a half an hour before the journey starts, and of course the dog should not have any food. Dogs get very thirsty and it is as well to break the journey half way and give them a drink. A plastic water container and bowl should always be included in your luggage.

I generally take an older dog with me who enjoys going in the car if I have to take puppies on a long journey. It gives them confidence. Something to amuse them like a large bone or a few hard biscuits helps to keep them occupied. I once found that a newspaper laid over the rug in case of accidents provided excellent entertainment for the whole of an hundred mile journey to the airport even though I arrived looking as though I had been to a wedding.

On journeys such as this it is most important that the puppy is not sick, as there is no knowing when the next meal will be forthcoming, if the puppy has a long flight before it.

Never tolerate bad behaviour in a car. If possible have a guard fixed so that they cannot jump forward on to the front seat.

Nothing is more distracting for a driver than a dog who is bouncing about backwards and forwards and from side to side.

Never in any circumstances should a dog be put in the boot of a car. I have seen this done so often, generally by shooting men who arrive at the meet in sleek cars with the dogs in the boot because they are afraid of them soiling the inside. It is illegal to put an animal in a travelling box so that it cannot stand up if you are sending it either by rail or by air, and yet dogs are made to crouch down in the boot of a car in complete darkness and travel for miles in this cramped position with fumes penetrating from the exhaust.

I can think of nothing more terrifying for any animal. I know of two instances where dogs have been put in the boot and forgotten. One man told me that his dog was missing for three days and he could not understand it until he remembered that it was in the boot of his car and locked in the garage. Another man thought it was a huge joke that he went off for the week-end and forgot his dog was in the boot. This sort of thing should be punishable by law. Unfortunately it is done all too often by people who should know better than to inflict this sort of cruelty on their animals.

It is important that owners of dogs should be warned not to leave dogs or puppies in cars without adequate ventilation and shade. It is surprising how careless, and indeed callous, people can be in this respect. Although a car may be parked in the shade it does not always mean that it will remain so if the owner is away for a long period and the sun moves round.

A car can quickly become an oven and many dogs are left by thoughtless owners to suffer from extreme exhaustion from which many die a terrible death.

These days it is possible to buy expanding window guards which can be inserted in the window and let down so that the dogs inside are able to benefit from all the air possible and still not be able to jump out. As an emergency precaution a car rug can be thrown over the roof of the car to cover the window affected by the sun but it is better still to leave all dogs at home during the hot weather if at all possible. They will be better off resting at home in shady runs or in a well ventilated house.

Air Travel

So many people seem to think that it is complicated to send a dog abroad. In fact, it is quite simple when you know how.

The first thing to do is to apply to the Ministry of Agriculture, Fisheries and Food, Government Buildings, Block B, Hook Rise South, Tolworth, Surbiton, Surrey, or telephone Derwent 6611 for the regulations applying to the country to which the puppy is to be sent. Each country has different restrictions but it is a simple matter to enquire and find out what they are. The Ministry will be able to give you all the up-to-date information and if a licence is found to be necessary they will send you the appropriate form to fill in.

You will then know at once whether the puppy has to be vaccinated with Rabies vaccine before export, or if he requires a blood test or any other stipulated requirement. An early enquiry can save delays later. Some countries offer more complications than others. Finland, for instance, requires a faeces test. Dogs sent to Denmark have to be accompanied by a statement sworn before a Commissioner of Oaths that they have not left the breeder's premises; and when I sent the first two Goldens ever to go to the Argentine, they had to be accompanied by passport photographs.

Apart from any necessary injections a Health Certificate must be obtained from a veterinary surgeon approved by the Ministry of Agriculture. This must be signed a stipulated number of days before the dog is exported, but to qualify for it the puppy may need some preliminary immunisation or treatment so it is as well to enquire some time in advance. A form on which to apply for an export pedigree must be obtained from the Kennel Club and returned with a fee. In the case of a male dog, the form must be signed by a veterinary surgeon as having examined the dog and found both testicles descended into the scrotum. If possible the export pedigree should be sent with the puppy but this is not absolutely necessary.

Book the puppy on a direct flight if possible wherever it is going. If you are not going to use an agent to send the puppy then a travelling box must either be obtained beforehand or arrangements made for it to be delivered to the cargo department of the airline being used. Travelling boxes are made in various sizes of light weight material to a specification laid down by the authorities and the box should be of a size which will allow the dog sufficient freedom and room to stand up and turn around.

Although I have done much of my own exporting in the past I think that nowadays it is better to use a good export agent of repute who will take care of all the details and provide the travelling box. They are experts at the job and will deliver the puppy to the airport and notify the purchaser in advance of the time of arrival. Sometimes a puppy or grown dog may be going on a long distance flight such as to Australia or New Zealand. This must be done through an agent as quarantine kennels have to be booked in the country to which the dog is going and a special kennel is required which is sealed before take-off and must not be opened until the animal is examined by the veterinary authorities on arrival. If the plane is delayed in any country during the journey and the kennel is opened, then the dog will have to be flown back to this country and put into quarantine kennels for six months.

If an agent is handling your puppy it can be delivered the day before the flight to his kennels. If he is a bad car traveller this will give him time to get over this part of the journey and allow him to have a good meal and sleep before taking off the next day, especially if you use an agent whose kennels are close to the airport.

If you are handling the puppy yourself and have either written or phoned the airline which you have decided to use they will have told you the flight number and airway bill number. Most airlines insist on payment at the time of despatch, but it is sometimes possible for payment to be made on arrival by the new owner if you give the airline the name and address of the person to whom the puppy is going about ten days prior to the flight.

All you have to do now is to arrive at the airport about three hours before the flight. This means rather a long wait so I have the puppy weighed in his travelling box, then take him out again and put him in the car while I go back and complete the necessary formalities.

It is generally possible to find a piece of grass near by on which to give the puppy a last minute run and I take with me some raw beef and a flask of egg and milk to give him before he finally goes back in the travelling box.

In case of an early morning flight, or an unexpected cancellation, arrangements can be made for the puppy to stay overnight at the R.S.P.C.A. kennels attached to the airport and be put on the flight the next day. Advance notice of this should be given if possible.

I have found on enquiry that the puppies and adults which I have sent on long journeys by air have arrived quite clean and in excellent spirits.

Some people recommend giving a tranquillizer before sending them off. I have never thought this to be necessary with a Golden Retriever but it is probably advisable with some very highly sensitive breeds.

One of the most amusing journeys by air on which I sent a dog was from our local airfield. I had an English Setter bitch on which I had spent a fortune using the best stud dogs available and each time the puppies faded out after a few days. I finally decided to give her away to an army officer who was involved in air reconnaisance and stationed about eighty miles away. He rang me up and asked me to meet him with the dog at the airfield. When I arrived I discovered that it was an open biplane. This took place some years ago. However, not the least disturbed, the bitch was placed on the back seat and with a complete air of disdain soared into the air like Dismal Desmond sitting on a magic carpet.

Somewhile later I heard that she had been accidentally mated to a Labrador and when the puppies arrived I went to see them. She had ten perfectly healthy black puppies none of which had any intention of fading out and this was the only really healthy litter she ever reared. I had managed to save one or two from earlier litters but it had been a heart breaking job seeing them die one after another.

3 Kennel Management and General Care

The most important thing in running a kennel of any breed of dog is to establish a routine and stick to it. I am a great believer in feeding and exercising at the same time every day. It seems to me that a dog expects so little in his life that it is only fair that the highlights of his day should come at regular hours, and not be put off, often till late at night, to suit the owner's convenience.

Adult dogs should have one meal a day, and the best time to give this is late afternoon. In winter the dogs can then have a last run out in the exercising yard or paddock and after that be shut up for the night.

I do not recommend that they should be disturbed again before morning. It is quite unnecessary and causes a lot of trouble to let them all out again last thing at night. If undisturbed they will go through the night until they are let out in the morning without soiling their kennel. This does not apply to puppies of course who in any case will be having a last feed.

Nor does it apply to house dogs. Even so they are very reluctant to leave their warm beds and judging by the speed of their return I doubt very much whether the purpose of their exit has been accomplished.

In the summer I like the dogs to have the benefit of all the daylight possible and they are not shut up until dark. They are let out about half past seven but in the winter they are not let out until daylight. I see no point in letting them out on cold wet winter mornings to stand about in their runs in the darkness.

It is a common practice usually amongst trainers, keepers and working kennels never to shut dogs up at all but to leave them to go in and out as they please. The type of exit is a pop hole similar to that used on a fowl house only bigger.

If this method is used, do not expect a visiting dog or bitch to your kennel who is accustomed to being shut in at night to go through a door of this kind of his own accord to sleep inside. He will probably be a bit upset in any case by being left and should be shut in his new quarters at night at any rate until he has become used to them.

I get a sense of satisfaction especially on cold wet nights to know that my dogs are all safely shut up. They jump up on their benches and wait for me to give each one a few hard biscuits before I shut the door.

And as I walk away I hear the rustle of straw and the contented crunching of biscuits, and I am happy to know that they are all well fed, well housed, and have a dry warm bed, unlike the unfortunate dogs who have to endure an appalling draught from an open door all night.

One way, however, of combatting some of the draughts if the open door method is used is to have a piece of double duty rubber the same size as the aperture and suspended from the top so that as the animal pushes against it, it will give way and fall back in place covering the exit as soon as the dog has gone through. This method is used extensively in America and Canada and I must say that I find it most useful myself for daytime use especially for young puppies.

In this case the puppies have an infra-red ray lamp inside suspended over their bed and they are free to run in and out all day. With tiny puppies the rubber is too heavy for them to push so I use a piece of carpet which is firm enough to fall back into place. Puppies soon get the idea and I must say they never dirty their kennel in the daytime when they can run outside, even in really bad weather, just for a minute or two to be clean. It is a good idea to arrange the bed so that

A litter under an infra-red lamp, with exit door to kennel fitted with flaps enabling puppies to go in and out while still ensuring a warm temperature inside the kennel.

there is a board about eighteen inches high on the side nearest the door which will act as a screen from any draught caused by the exit.

Bedding

Bedding can be of a good wheat straw, woodwool or shavings, some people like to use deep sawdust, but on no account use hay which harbours parasites.

If straw is used it should be changed about once a week as it becomes broken down and dusty. It can then be either burnt or put on a compost heap. Woodwool is excellent but is expensive and I find that burning is the only way of disposing of it. Shavings are also quite good but they do not, to my mind, afford the same amount of comfort in the winter. They are quite satisfactory in the summer and are in fact preferable to straw during August and September which are the worst months for fleas, lice, and harvest bugs. Some summers seem worse than others in this respect and dogs exercised over hay fields and stubble ground will very easily pick up one or other of these insects, so a constant dusting with insecticide during these months is advisable. It is also as well to dust the beds with insecticide before fresh straw is put down, and occasionally they should be scrubbed with disinfectant.

Sawdust is absolutely necessary on every kennel floor as it helps to soak up the moisture brought in on dogs' feet, and so avoids the bedding getting wet through constant running in and out. In the case of puppies it helps enormously in cleaning up excrement.

Sawdust is sometimes used as bedding in which case it should be several inches thick in the sleeping box.

Kennel Runs

The size of your runs depends on the amount of land you have available but I suggest that they be made as large as possible and if space will allow, they should lead out into an exercising area which is safely fenced in.

This is such an asset that I would sacrifice a little on the size of the kennel runs, in order to incorporate it in my kennel layout.

Kennel runs can be made from concrete, bricks or hard core, of which there are several kinds such as coke, clinker, or gravel. Although I have seen the last two in use, I do not favour either of them as they are not easily cleaned and present quite a hazard for young dogs and puppies who invariably pick up stones and small pieces of clinker which they can crunch and easily swallow.

My vet showed me an X-ray once of a small dog who had swallowed so many stones that he rattled when picked up. This has always made me very careful about leaving anything around which puppies might swallow, as they seem to take a delight, even in grass runs, in digging holes and finding something to chew.

I think that the advantages of concrete runs far out-weigh the disadvantages. They are easily cleaned and disinfected and if laid with a slight fall they will drain quickly and dry out. I provide a low table to each run so that the dogs can jump up and lie down on it if they wish. This also serves other useful purposes as it is less painful to groom the dogs on a table than to stoop down to their level. They quickly learn to jump up without hesitation and this used to be a great asset in the old days when dogs had to be passed by the vet at shows, as they jumped on the table with great delight. Concrete runs should be sprayed daily in the summer with disinfectant and hosed down if necessary. In winter this is not often the case owing to frequent rain, and brushing is all that they need.

Grass runs are difficult to keep clean and get foul after a time as well as becoming a quagmire of mud in the winter. Of course if you have a fenced in paddock it is different but for kennel runs I do not think that grass is practical as the ground can become infected by bacteria and virus such as *coccidiosis* which will keep on recurring unless the ground is rested and treated with a dressing of lime. On no account should it be used for at least six weeks after application.

If dogs are constantly running on soft ground their nails may need filing or even clipping. This is not a job for the amateur as nails clipped with a blunt instrument or clipped too close to the quick can cause a lot of pain. Clipping baby puppy's nails is a different matter as they are not nearly so strong and hard.

I find that one of the advantages of concrete runs is that feet and nails are kept in excellent condition as the nails are worn right back with constant running up and down. Road walking does help in this respect and is in fact essential if the runs do not have a hard surface.

Fencing

For small runs railings can be used or prefabricated wire panels can be bought for this purpose. But chain linked fencing is most suitable for fencing in a large area. It must be properly erected with straining wire top and bottom otherwise it will sag and go out of shape. If the run is concrete and the straining wire really taut it will be difficult for a dog to lever his way underneath it, but a single row of concrete blocks around the outside edge will make it doubly secure. If, however, the wire is surrounding a grass run it should be trenched into the ground about six inches to prevent burrowing underneath.

The height of the wire should be not less than six feet. It is a wise precaution to have a foot of wire sloping inwards at the top to deter those dogs who have a knack of climbing to get out. On the whole I find that dogs who are brought up in kennels and are happy in their environment have no inclination to get out. But with boarders and visiting bitches it is a different matter, and every care must be taken to see that they do not escape. Be sure that you have good gate fasteners as some Goldens are very clever at opening doors and gates, even to turning knobs and lifting latches. For this reason I have a bolt as well as a fastener.

It is quite surprising how people unused to animals blithely walk through gates without closing them, whereas it becomes second nature to shut a gate after you have lived with animals all your life. I find tradesmen and postmen are the worst offenders. It just does not seem to occur to them to shut the gate even though they can see dogs loose in the garden. On one occasion many years ago when my husband and I had gone out for the evening some members of the local youth club were using our tennis court and sent a ball into one of my dog runs where there were about six dogs at the time. Without thinking one of them opened the gate and went in leaving it wide open and all the dogs streamed out into an adjoining lane.

When the youngsters realised what had happened they pursued the dogs down the lane shouting to a pedestrian to head them off. The result was that as the dogs reached the bridge which spans the main trunk road someone stood in the middle waving his arms madly to stop them.

A young bitch of mine about a year old leapt on to the parapet of the bridge and then fell twenty-five feet into the centre of the main road on an August Bank holiday. It was a wonder she did not land on a car and how she missed being run over I do not know. Even twenty years ago the traffic was bad enough, on bank holiday in particular. However, she dragged herself into the side of the road and remained there until I arrived home. I was telephoned at a friend's house and I told them not to move her until I got there. You can imagine my feelings. Needless to say the youth club no longer use our tennis court!

X-rays showed that the bitch had a broken sacrum and my vet said that he could do nothing for her. She was quite helpless and could not stand up at all. After several anxious days we decided to drive her to London to the Royal Veterinary College and get a second opinion. We need not have bothered. The verdict was the same. Nothing could be done. We were told that time would tell and that in all probability the bone would heal in about three weeks during which time she must be allowed to lie as still as possible.

I shall never forget that three weeks. My husband and I lifted her on to a hearth rug and at regular intervals carried her on the rug out of doors where she made every effort to be clean. Gradually she put more weight on her hind-quarters and it was just like a miracle when at the end of three weeks she could stand up. Every day she grew stronger until she was back to normal but the accident left a permanent twitch in her hind leg where a nerve had been damaged beyond repair. She was able to have two or three litters without trouble but the twitch, which was most pronounced, stayed with her for the rest of her life.

Kennels

Kennels need not be elaborate but above all they must be dry, with adequate space and enough light and ventilation. Over the years I have seen dogs kept under all sorts of conditions and one of the worst kinds of cruelty is to keep dogs shut up in small kennels during very hot weather.

I once saw a Golden shut up in a house made from corrugated iron which when opened resembled an oven more than anything else. Corrugated iron roofs are waterproof but they are also hot in summer and cold in winter and if used should be insulated. Asbestos kennels are quite good and are certainly hard-wearing but they tend to be very cold in winter.

There is much to be said for a wooden kennel and I think that on the whole these are the most popular. There are many firms who specialise in dog kennels and kennel equipment. Most of the kennels are fitted with bench-type beds inside and some have runs adjoining. Most wooden kennels have felt roofs which are very good but do have to be watched for leaks and the felt replaced every four to five years. Very often I have found that ready made kennels are too flimsy and are only suitable for small breeds. For this reason I have used pig houses and find them more successful as they are made from heavier tongued and grooved wood and have more substantial fittings. It is surprising how much damage dogs can do to a kennel. Sometimes through sheer mischievousness they will gnaw the edge of a door or corner of a house and I have known a visiting bitch to eat her way right through the side of a kennel during the night. Some stud dogs work themselves up into a state of great excitement when there are bitches in season and will do a lot of damage to a kennel.

I like the kennels to be high enough to stand up in as it is very back aching to brush out a kennel in a semi-stooping position. They should be big enough if possible to accommodate two dogs at least. I never like kennelling one dog on its own if it can be avoided. Some people are fortunate enough to have good outbuildings which can be adapted and made into excellent kennels. Usually these take the form of loose boxes or cow stalls. In either case they can be sectioned off in a row to kennel a number of dogs either separately or together with a door in front of each section and a passage running down the length of the block. This is a method used frequently in boarding kennels where a number of dogs can be kept under one roof. It may be necessary to put a false ceiling if the building is very high and draughty. If not, the bed should be made with a lid or canopy to keep the heat generated by the dog from rising.

Even more cosy is a small kennel or large travelling box, like those used for air travel, with a front opening, but you must be sure that the dog does go into it at night and does not lie about on the stone floor. If brought up to use a bed of this kind it is all right but do not expect a new dog or visitor unaccustomed to sleeping quarters of this kind to use it. Without doubt he or she will spend the night curled up on the floor rather than venture into it. For this reason I give each dog a few hard biscuits when I put them to bed and insist that they are sitting up on their beds before they get them. In this way I am fairly sure that they sleep in their beds. Never give a dog a bone when you shut him up, as it is just possible that he may get into difficulties and need assistance.

It is a wise precaution to see that all windows are covered with either strong netting or bars. I once had a whippet who seemed to suffer from claustrophobia so we could never keep him shut up. As a result, he was known in all the villages around and we had complaints about his wandering habits. Fortunately, there was not as much traffic then as there is today. To endeavour to stop him going off we fed him in a stable where he had a very comfortable bed, and shut him in. He had been in the habit of coming and going as he pleased on account of his obvious dislike of being shut in and the noise he made to demonstrate this. On this occasion it was not long before we heard a loud crash and rushed out to find that he had jumped clean through a high window. It was hardly believable that he could have jumped so high and even more so that he was hardly scratched.

If you do use a stable to rear a litter, do not do what I have so often seen done. That is: to cover the whole floor with deep straw. In this way the puppies learn to foul the straw, as they have nowhere else to go and no set place to sleep. A bad habit of this kind is very hard to cure and then nothing is more annoying than to have a dog who deliberately goes into his bed to relieve himself, with the result that the bedding is constantly wet.

I once bought an English Setter and it seemed that nothing we could do would stop him from wetting his bed until at last we put straw inside sacks and placed them on his sleeping bench; it worked like a charm. I mention this as I have heard of Golden owners having similar trouble, no doubt due to bad early training as most Goldens train very easily and are by nature exceptionally clean.

Where straw is strewn over the entire floor it is usually done to save labour as fresh straw is piled on top instead of the dirty material being removed daily. Not only does it encourage bad habits but it is very bad for the puppies' feet. One generally sees this method used on farms where straw is in abundance.

If you have the room I would recommend that the whelping kennel should be placed away from all the other dogs as a bitch at this time should be kept as quiet and undisturbed as possible. This should be large enough to accommodate a whelping box of 4 ft by 3 ft and leave plenty of room for the puppies to run about when they are older. It must have electricity so that an infra-red lamp can be suspended over the bed, and also have a good sized window which can be opened if necessary.

Be sure that the electrical installation is absolutely correct as one hears from time to time so many distressing stories of farm and kennel fires where large numbers of animals are destroyed. Not many years ago a Golden Retriever breeder lost her own life trying to rescue her dogs from a fire of this kind. In her memory the Golden Retriever Club raised a fund which was put towards surgical instruments to equip the Small Animal Health Trust Research Centre at Kennet, Cambridge.

General Diet

The daily diet should be made up chiefly of protein and carbohydrates. There are many alternative forms in which the protein can be fed. Red meat, tripe, sheep's paunch or sheep's head, fish, rabbit or tinned meat are the ones usually available, as well as eggs.

One must be guided by the supply in the area in which one lives and choose a form of meat which can be relied upon for a regular supply.

In some areas it is possible to get good raw meat and where this is possible I am sure it is to be preferred, but very often tripe is the only alternative and is widely used in kennels today as it is more economically priced. But it is not pleasant to handle and requires some preparation if collected direct from the slaughter house, as it generally contains a great deal of surplus fat and needs thorough washing. Where neither of these can be obtained, tinned meat is probably the only answer. This is expensive to use in a large kennel but a great deal of time is saved. Frozen meat or frozen meat with cereal added is popular and available in most districts. Herrings make a good change of diet but they must be cooked in a pressure cooker so that the bones become quite soft. Rabbit also makes a tempting dish for an invalid or a sick puppy but it must be cooked and carefully boned. Dehydrated meat is generally relished as a change but must not be given too liberally as it will cause scouring if over done.

In recent years there has come on the market a complete dog food which is used in some kennels with success. It is a balanced diet and needs no preparation so that a great deal of time is saved but it is quite expensive. Personally I do not favour its use as to me it seems unnatural and certainly most uninteresting. I cannot imagine anyone living on a bottle of tablets each day and relishing it as much as a beef steak, nor do I believe that a dog enjoys a dish of pellets as much as a pound of beef. If there is nothing else for him to eat I am prepared to accept that most dogs will in the end eat it. The thought of hopper-feeding litters of puppies is something which I cannot agree with. It is a well known scientific fact that a dog's character is formed within the first eight to ten weeks of its life. He needs human contact and he needs to feel secure and wanted. The idea of rearing a litter so impersonally as to hopper-feed them like a litter of pigs is quite repugnant to me. However, it is done and no doubt this habit will increase particularly where time is money, but the puppies will grow up to be characterless robots. Fortunately most Golden Retriever breeders are very attached to their dogs but one should always be on the watch for the puppy farmer who may well adopt these methods, and every care should be taken to see that puppies are only sold to people of good repute with adequate means and facilities.

Biscuit meal is the usual source of carbohydrates although there are other meals on the market. It should be well soaked but not allowed to be soggy. A crumbly consistency is best and I prefer to use fine biscuit meal for adults as well as puppies. It soaks quickly and is just as economical and the dogs seem to eat it more readily. On no account should terrier or hound meal be given unless it has been soaked for about two hours otherwise it will be hard in the middle and swell up inside the dog causing indigestion.

Some people prefer to feed biscuit dry particularly to those breeds with harsh coats but for Golden Retrievers I believe the best results are when it is given soaked. I give hard biscuits as a morning feed and a few at bedtime. When it is possible to add green vegetables to the diet this should be done as well as root vegetables which can be grated raw. Chives can be chopped and added to the meal and onions boiled with the tripe if this is cooked. I like to feed it raw when it is fresh but as it does not keep very well it is sometimes better to cook it. It is never necessary to add fat to the diet if tripe is fed as there is always sufficient included.

FOOD PROPORTIONS

I believe that environment plays a large part in the well-being of a dog and there is no hard and fast rule as to the exact amount of food which should be given to any one dog to keep him in good health.

The conditions under which dogs are kept, the local climate, and I believe to some extent the water which they drink, have some bearing on their development as on that of cattle and horses.

It is noticeable that a puppy from one litter sent to a different part of the country differs completely from his litter mates when grown up. Some kennels seem to produce large animals no matter how they are reared whilst others continually produce smaller types. I may be wrong but I have seen it happen so many times that I am convinced that growth is prompted not only by the food intake but is also influenced by the mineral content of the water and climatic conditions.

For my own part I am aware that I feed my dogs very heavily compared to some kennels. Although it is not as cold in the south-west as in many parts of the country, my dogs are unavoidably exposed to the south-west winds and a great deal of rain. Under these conditions they require more carbohydrates in the form of biscuit meal to keep them in condition than dogs kept in a sheltered position or even in the house. Such dogs would probably require only half the amount of biscuit meal as they are not burning up energy to keep warm and would quickly put on fat if not kept on a high protein diet. On average I would say that a pound of meat a day and half a pound of biscuit meal would suit most adult Goldens.

I remember going on a circuit of shows with some friends in America and I was rather surprised to note that they took with them sufficient water for the trip rather than let the dogs drink water from a different source, in case it should upset them. It is understandable when such vast distances are covered that this could happen. Rather like getting 'Mediterranean tummy' when we go abroad.

THE IMPORTANCE OF VITAMINS

Since dogs have been deprived through domestication of their natural sources of vitamins it is necessary that their diet should be balanced in order to maintain good health. Although I am not a great believer in spending small fortunes on pills and potions as some breeders do, firmly believing that this money is better spent on good natural food such as meat, eggs, milk and wholemeal biscuit, there are times when I think such additives are justified. One such occasion is when a bitch is in whelp and during lactation. Extra calcium is of obvious benefit when a bitch is called upon to reproduce good bone formation in her offspring. Generally speaking good fresh food contains all the health giving vitamins without the necessity of adding more, which in any event can upset the ratio of those already present in the diet.

Vitamin A which is contained in egg yolk encourages growth in puppies and improves the coat of adults by giving it a healthy gloss. It is also found in animal fat so that a dog should not be fed on a diet of lean meat entirely, particularly in winter when more energy producing food is required to keep up the body temperature. Extra fat can be added to the normal diet with advantage particularly if the dog is a 'bad doer' and would be improved with a little more weight. A lump of suet bought from a butcher and grated into the biscuit meal is a palatable way of feeding it.

Vitamin A is also present in milk so that egg and milk fed to bitches in whelp and to weaned puppies promotes growth at a time when it is most needed.

Vitamin B is also found in eggs, milk, meat, and yeast and this is necessary to help digestion and strengthen the nervous system. A little raw baker's yeast added to the diet of a nervous animal can be of great benefit.

Vitamin C is the one found in grass and vegetables which is probably why dogs eat it with such relish on occasions and should be allowed to do so. Even their fondness for eating cowdung and other things such as coal is nature's way of providing extra vitamins so necessary for their well-being.

I have heard of dogs, which have been lost in the country for long periods, having kept themselves alive by eating cowdung when nothing else has been available.

Vitamin D is promoted by sunshine and as for human beings it is necessary for good health and growth. Kennels and runs should be situated where they are likely to catch as much sunlight as possible, especially in this country where we never seem to get enough of it. Vitamin D is also found in eggs and I find it beneficial to use them liberally in my kennel, especially for puppies as it prevents rickets and other deficiencies. Cod liver oil and halibut oil are also rich in Vitamin D.

Vitamin E is associated with fertility and it is very often a lack of this which causes infertility. It is present in wholemeal biscuit which also provides the necessary carbohydrates to keep the digestion functioning naturally. Wheat germ oil capsules may be given with good results where infertility is caused by insufficient Vitamin E. Cod liver oil is one of the best ways of adding Vitamins A and D to the diet as both are found in fish oils and help in the development of healthy bone to prevent rickets. Although cod liver oil is the usual way of adding Vitamin A to the diet it should not be done indiscriminately as too much will destroy the Vitamin E content of the diet and infertility will result. Many people add liberal amounts of cod liver oil or Halibut oil to the diets of adults without realising their folly, especially if only a small amount of biscuit meal is fed, as this is the natural source of Vitamin E.

I am a great believer in feeding raw eggs but although dogs do not derive any direct benefit from the white of the egg neither does it appear to do any harm. Many people separate it from the yolk but I never do and have never seen any harmful results for so doing. It is, however, the yolk which contains the vitamins which form such a necessary part of the dog's diet.

Grooming

Most dogs like being groomed as this calls for extra personal attention and fussing over which they love.

From puppyhood they have learnt the drill and roll over on their backs so that tummy feathering can be brushed out and any knots removed.

I like to set aside a regular time each week to examine each dog carefully, checking teeth, ears, coat and claws.

Teeth can be descaled if necessary by your vet but I have never found this necessary. I think that bones and hard biscuit help to keep teeth in good condition.

Ears can be a problem if not watched and a regular dusting with canker powder helps to keep them in good order. If neglected a dirty ear will soon smell badly and a chronic condition will soon follow.

It is caused by a mite which cannot generally be seen but it is surprising how quickly it will spread from one dog to another if not checked.

Coats should be brushed but I do not advise too much combing as it does tend to break the long feathering on legs and tail.

If dogs scratch there is always a reason so look for the cause. Fleas can be detected by the dirt they leave in the coat usually on the back and base of the tail which are their favourite places. Lice are also a nuisance but are easily got rid of with insecticide if not neglected and allowed to get established in the beds. Puppies are the chief culprits and should be dusted regularly. I never allow puppies to sleep on straw for this reason but prefer sacking which can be washed out in disinfectant. One can easily acquire large pieces of hessian from carpet dealers which have been used as wrappers. These cut up into smaller pieces and hemmed around to prevent fraying make most useful bedding for puppies and can be easily washed or left to soak in a bath of disinfectant.

Lice are often located round the ears and chest of puppies but seldom seem to affect older dogs.

If you exercise your dogs where sheep have been it is possible that they may pick up a tick from time to time, especially during the summer. These bite deep into the skin and suck the blood. When you find one you may at first think that it is a wart. They are like tiny bladders filled with blood and look blue-grey in colour. To remove it a firm hold should be taken as close to the skin as possible and a sharp pull will dislodge it. Dispose of it as quickly as possible underfoot and dab the spot where it has been with antiseptic.

Exercising

As already mentioned I firmly believe that this should be at the same time every day. Regular habits are quickly formed and a dog will look forward to his daily outing and settle down contentedly afterwards.

I do not feel that one can definitely say exactly how far or how long exercising should take, as it entirely depends on the circumstances under which the dogs are kept.

A very large proportion of dog breeders who only keep a small number of dogs do not have the facilities for exercising on their own premises, in which case they must be walked on a lead or taken to a park or field. If possible the dogs should have some freedom to run. Obviously the less freedom they have at home the further they must be walked. Unfortunately far too many dogs do not get enough free exercise to stretch their legs and harden their muscles. I know that walking is a tremendous help in that it tightens feet, strengthens pasterns and generally helps to tighten up the muscles; even so I do not think that the average person can walk fast enough to really do a lot of good without some free ranging as well. A bicycle is excellent for exercising dogs but unfortunately in these days it is not very practical owing to increased traffic. At one time I always cycled daily with five or six dogs loose. You can regulate your speed so that the dogs step out at a really good quick walk, not a gallop. Of all methods I think this is the most beneficial unless you are fortunate enough to be able to exercise them on horseback. However, these methods are only recommended to those people who are sufficiently isolated for it to be safe from traffic.

I do not like the practice of dogs being exercised behind cars. This is highly dangerous and the dog is not under control and it is simply a lazy man's way of avoiding walking. It cannot be much fun for the dog either.

I am sure that during the winter in particular many dogs suffer by being confined to house or kennel whilst the owners are at work and probably do not return until dark. It is not sufficient to take them for long and exhausting walks at the week-ends and leave them shut up in small runs all the week. It is the regularity not the distance which counts.

I believe that we should see far better movement in the ring if exercising were taken more seriously. Puppies should be included at about five months onward. I repeat that a marathon is not necessary and certainly not for puppies. In the case of puppies if you have plenty of space and a fenced in field you may not need to do more than let them romp around at will. Even so I find that they are apt to return to the kennels if not actually accompanied and wait for someone to go with them. Personally I enjoy the pleasure of taking them loose across the fields every morning.

Goldens in the Home

Many Goldens live as family pets from an early age, but there are a few things to bear in mind when rearing a puppy in the home, especially during his first year.

Like his kennel-reared brothers and sisters he needs a balanced diet, a consistent routine, and sufficient company and attention. I am continually surprised by enquiries from people who think a puppy can be left to himself all day until they have time for him in the evening. This is not ideal even for a grown dog, and it is certainly no way to treat a puppy.

When picking up a puppy do be sure to support him underneath. Do not lift him by his elbows and leave the rest of him to dangle, which is something I have often seen. He should be put down gently, supporting him until he is safely on his feet.

If he has the run of the garden make sure that he cannot find a way out when he feels like exploring. When he is old enough for exercise outside his own territory he should of course always be accompanied. Hard-surface walking will toughen his feet and build up muscle tone, but this should not begin too early in life or it can do more harm than good. Rough play with larger dogs should never be allowed as it often leads to injuries.

A problem in the home is that of stairs. It is not good for a puppy or young dog to be continually up and down them. He may not actually dislocate a joint but proper development can be affected, resulting in later weakness. The pet puppy may not be a show dog but he will be all the more rewarding in the long run if he is carefully reared from the beginning.

4 Showing and Judging

Choosing a Show

I am often asked by people who have never shown a dog how they can find out where shows are being held and how to obtain the schedules.

As with any hobby, in the first place you will want to learn as much as possible about the 'dog game' and show procedure so it is advisable to take one or both of the weekly periodicals which are devoted solely to dog breeding and showing. These are *Dog World* and *Our Dogs*.

Not only are the shows advertised in the papers but they contain many interesting and helpful articles as well as a column devoted to Golden Retrievers and critiques on the winning dogs at most of the shows.

Much can be learnt by reading these reports, especially if you have been fortunate enough to have had a winning dog at a previous show. Most exhibitors are anxious to find out exactly what the judge thought of their dog and why he placed him first, second or third.

The Golden Retriever column is written by Mrs Stonex in *Our Dogs* and Mrs Tudor in *Dog World*. Both give items of interest about the breed each week and if you follow these closely you will soon become aware of what is going on in the breed, and of important wins in other parts of the country and overseas.

From the shows advertised you will be able to choose which ones you wish to go to, and you should write to the secretary and ask for the schedule of the show being organised by that society.

The whole of the British Isles is well covered by Specialist Breed Clubs for Golden Retrievers and you would be well advised to become a member of the one which covers your area. As you become more interested and more successful you will want to branch out and join other clubs and societies, each of which will hold shows throughout the year. Most Specialist Breed Clubs hold one Championship Show each year and if you are a member you will become eligible to compete for the club's trophies and many other advantages.

Information about the Specialist Breed Club to cover your district may be obtained from *The Golden Retriever Club,* Hon.Sec. Mrs

Theed, Squirrels Brook, Salter's Green, Mayfield, Sussex. Telephone Rotherfield 2509.

The United Retriever Club, which covers all types of Retriever, organises Working Tests and Training Classes as well as promoting Shows and Field Trials. The Club has many branches throughout the country and the honorary secretary for your area will be pleased to furnish any information you may require about local activities. Details of your area branch can be obtained from *The United Retriever Club,* Hon.Sec. D.E. Compton Esq., Fox Close, Stoneley, Huntington. Telephone Kimbolton 664.

Making an Entry for a Show

Having obtained the schedule you should read the definition of the classes very carefully and decide which your dog is eligible to enter for. Wherever possible choose shows which cater for the breed with several classes and a specialist gundog judge, rather than a variety show where there are no classes for Golden Retrievers separately classified, and the judge is what is known as an all-rounder.

Ch. Camrose Cabus Christopher. By Ch. Camrose Tallyrand of Anbria ex Cabus Boltby Charmer. Owned by Mrs Tudor.

Ch. Stolford Happy
Lad. By Stolford
Playboy ex Prystina of
Wymondham.
Owned by Mrs P.
Robertson.

It is very often confusing for the beginner to know which are the best classes for him to enter his dog in and if possible he should take advice from a more experienced person.

If you have a puppy which is six months old and not more than twelve months old you can enter him for the Golden Retriever puppy class, the Gundog puppy class and the Any Variety puppy class. If you think your chances are very good and your puppy is well grown you may be tempted to enter him in the Novice or Maiden classes or even the Junior class if there is one scheduled. It is better, in my view, to stick to puppy classes to begin with and if you are successful you will then have the pleasure of coming into the ring to compete for the Trophy or Diploma for Best Puppy in Show which is an award of considerable merit. If you have been over ambitious and entered your puppy in several breed classes, even if you win the puppy class it is unlikely that he will be placed at the top in all the other classes and a lot of fees can be wasted by injudicious entries.

As wins in puppy classes do not count when entering in other classes such as Maiden or Novice, it is often better to keep a puppy out of these classes for another reason. If you should win two or three first prizes whilst your dog is still quite young you are penalising yourself in the long run because when you want to enter in stiffer competition at a Championship Show you will find that he or she is not eligible for Maiden or Novice and is probably not mature enough to enter in Undergraduate or Graduate classes.

Of course, most people are happy to receive a card of any colour, particularly if the competition is very strong, so you should not feel too discouraged if your dog gets picked out at all. The first prize card is red, the second prize card is blue and the third is yellow. There is usually a Reserve card and sometimes a prize to go with it, and a white card for the Very Highly Commended, which is fifth place.

At some Championship Shows where there are a great many entries, Highly Commended and Commended cards are also given.

Ch. Westley Jacquetta. By Ch. Crouchers Leo ex Samantha of Westley. Owned by Miss J. Gill and Mrs D. Philpott.

On the entry form which you have received with your schedule, you will be required to write in the registered name of the dog, his age, sex and the names of his parents as well as the classes you have selected. Send this with your entry fees before the closing date to the secretary and before the date of the show you will receive your exhibitor's pass. If you enter three dogs it is usual to receive two free passes. The other one is for a kennel maid or helper.

You will also be expected to sign the following declaration which you should read carefully and understand before doing so.

DECLARATION

I undertake to abide by the Rules and Regulations of the Kennel Club and of this show and I declare that the dogs entered have not suffered from or been exposed to the risk of Distemper or any contagious disease including febrile reaction to immunisation during the six weeks prior to exhibition and I will not show them if they incur such risks between now and the day of the show or if they have been immunised within fourteen days prior to the show. I declare that the dogs are not (1) totally blind, (2) afflicted with any condition which in the opinion of the Committee of the Kennel Club is hereditary and deleterious, (3) defective in hearing, (4) if a dog, castrated or prevented from breeding as a result of surgical operation, except that this shall not apply to a bitch that has progeny registered at the Kennel Club, (5) not entire (an entire dog is one which has two apparently normal testicles both descended and in the scrotum). Castrated dogs and spayed bitches are permitted to compete in Obedience Tests.

Types of Shows

There are several types of shows and it is as well to become acquainted with these and regulations governing them before entering for your first show.

Exemption Show

This type of show is so called because the dogs entered do not necessarily have to be registered at the Kennel Club. There are only four pedigree classes allowed but an unlimited number of Novelty Classes are permissible and very often two obedience classes are scheduled. They are usually organised in conjunction with some other function to raise money for charity and are not taken too seriously by breeders as awards won at this type of show do not count when entering for a Kennel Club licensed show.

They very often draw a large number of entries and are good practice for an inexperienced dog and as they usually include a child handlers class the whole family can join in and it makes a pleasant afternoon's entertainment.

Sanction Show

This type of show is run for the benefit of members only of the society or club organising it. It is an unbenched show and is confined to twenty classes unless it is run by a breed club in which case ten classes are the limit which can be scheduled and in either case no dog is eligible over the Post-Graduate standard.

Limited Show

This type of show is so named because it is limited in the number of classes which can be scheduled. It is also restricted to members of the society promoting the show within a restricted radius.

Challenge Certificate winners are not allowed to enter for competition. This type of show is always unbenched.

Open Shows

Open Shows have no restrictions on the number of type of classes scheduled and all dogs are eligible from any part of the country. It cannot be a benched show unless more than sixty classes have been scheduled. At the larger Open Shows it is usual to have several classes for each breed as at a Championship Show. Open Shows are very popular during the summer held in conjunction with Agricultural Shows or other out door events such as Horse Trials.

Championship Shows

Championship Shows cater for a wide variety of breeds and each breed has a classification which varies according to the popularity of the breed. Golden Retrievers are one of the most popular breeds and consequently most Championship Shows provide a large number of classes in the schedule. The Kennel Club offer Challenge Certificates for the best dog and the best bitch in each breed with the exception of a few uncommon breeds which have not had sufficient dogs registered at the Kennel Club to warrant awarding Challenge Certificates at any or all Championship Shows.

Some of the most important Championship Shows are spread over two or three days. Most Breed Clubs run their own Championship Show each year but this takes only one day.

Since it has become necessary to qualify a dog at a Championship Show by winning a first or second prize before it can be entered at Cruft's, the entries have gone up by leaps and bounds. In a popular breed like the Golden Retriever it has meant that frequently the numbers in some of the classes have been anything between thirty to thirty-five and on some occasions as many as forty. It is no mean feat in a breed as popular as this to make a dog or bitch into a Champion.

Making a Champion

The title of Champion is granted by the Kennel Club if a dog or bitch has gained three Challenge Certificates under three different judges and has proved himself in the field by winning not less than a Certificate of Merit at a Field Trial or gaining a Qualifying Certificate. In order to do this the dog has to be taken to a Field Trial where at least two judges on the 'A' judging list are officiating. The dog has to be in the line off the leash whilst birds are being shot so that it can be seen if he shows any sign of being gun-shy. He is then asked to pick one of the shot birds and retrieve tenderly to hand. It is not essential for the dog to be steady on this occasion but it is always better if he is. A dog can take a Qualifying Certificate after having won his first Challenge Certificate but not before. If he fails he cannot have more than three attempts and not more than twice in one shooting season. The Kennel Club have recently made a new rule which allows anybody who has won a first prize at a Championship Show to qualify his dog at a trial specially organised for this purpose. He is not permitted to qualify his dog at any other trial until he has won a Challenge Certificate.

SHOW CHAMPION
This is a title given to dogs or bitches which have won three Challenge Certificates under three different judges but have not won a Field Trial award or Qualifying Certificate.

FIELD TRIAL CHAMPION
This title refers to dogs who have won two first prizes at Open or All Aged Stakes one of which must be a variety Stake for all breeds of Retrievers or if he wins the Retriever Championship Stake. It is interesting to note that in Ireland the dog also has to have won a first, second or third at a show in order to gain the title of Irish Field Trial Champion.

DUAL CHAMPION
In order to become a Dual Champion which is the highest award, the dog has to become a Field Trial Champion as well as a Champion at the shows.

OBEDIENCE CHAMPION
There have, I believe, been only two Golden Retrievers who have gained this title in Great Britain. One is Obed. Ch. Castelnau Pizzicato

Sh. Ch. Concord of Yeo. By Ch. Stolford Happy Lad ex Ch. Deerflite Endeavour of Yeo. Owned by Mrs Lucille Sawtell.

Sh. Ch. Trident of Yeo Colbar. By Sh. Ch. Concord of Yeo ex Sweet Klarin (by Int. Ch. Mandingo Buidhe Colum). Owned by Mrs B. Keighley.

by Ch. Camrose Fantango out of Castelnau Concerto and bred by Miss Baker. The other is Obed. Ch. Nicholas of Albesdon by Stubblesdown Nerula out of Judy of Eglesfield and bred by Mr Forst.

In America and Canada a great deal of Obedience training is done by Golden Retrievers and it is considered to be a great attribute to have a dog with an Obedience title. In Great Britain, however, it is not as popular as Working Tests which are run along the lines of Field Trials but with dummies instead of live game. Obedience work is very much more automatic and precise whilst working tests train a dog to use his brains and teach him the job for which he was initially bred.

To gain the title of Obedience Champion the dog has to win three Obedience Challenge Certificates under three different judges but to win the Obedience Challenge Certificate at Cruft's automatically gives him the title. Only dogs which have won an Obedience Challenge Certificate during the previous year can compete. The Certificate is not awarded if the winning dog loses more than ten points during the competition. In this way the standard is kept very high and often only half points are lost.

Judging

If judging meant allocating points for each feature of the dog placed before you and adding them up, the end result would be odd indeed.

It is the duty of the judge to take into consideration the whole appearance of the animal and ask oneself if it is balanced, soundly constructed, moves correctly, has the kindly expression which it should have, and gives the impression of a workmanlike animal for which purpose it is bred. A heavily loaded dog would neither have the speed nor the endurance required for work in the field and this must not be lost sight of in the final analysis. The pretty eye-catching animal is not necessarily the best suited for this purpose. Nor is the highly excitable or nervous one. These points must also be taken into consideration.

TYPE

Type varies considerably in the breed although this is less noticeable in recent years.

The judge should have a clear picture in his mind of the type of dog he considers as near perfection in his opinion and approach each class with this in mind so that his final placings are all of one type.

Colour is of no great importance provided it is within the standard. Correct conformation is what one is looking for. One often hears at the ringside the remark that so and so is putting up all pale dogs or dark dogs as the case may be. Inevitably each judge has his own considered standard of perfection, consequently a certain shade of colouring may predominate in the final placing. Some dogs are more heavily boned than others. A few are too heavily so, but generally speaking there are far more lightly boned specimens which have nothing to pass on to the next generation and if bred from will only produce finer bone still. Even the best rearing will not produce good bone if it is not inherent in the puppy.

So when judging one should try to find a happy medium. Ample bone with quality and no sign of coarseness whilst lack of bone and substance should be penalised.

Some types are higher on the leg than others and whilst one deplores the racy type of Golden there is a tendency towards short legs and heavy bodies, which again is not consistent with a working dog. An active, strongly built well balanced dog with an intelligent and kindly expression is what one should look for.

Although soundness is of great importance type should not be sacrificed.

I have never forgotten words of wisdom from a well-known judge many years ago who said, 'even a mongrel can be sound'. What good is a perfectly sound dog if he lacks all the characteristics of the breed he represents? It is the elusive combination of both which makes breeders go on breeding and ultimately establish a strain and type of their own.

Ch. Royal Pal Catcombe. By Mandingo Beau Geste of Yeo ex Patsy Adams. Owned by Mr and Mrs D. Andrews.

CONFORMATION

Heads vary considerably and often betray quite clearly the line from which they have descended. As the standard says they should have a broad skull with powerful muzzle and good stop. Too often we see the lack of stop and the snipy jaw but this has improved in recent years. I am glad to say that eyes too are very much better and a really light eye is seldom seen. Equally a hard expression is not desirable nor should the haw be apparent. The rim of the eye should be dark in colour and fit closely round the eye neither turning in nor sagging and giving a houndy look.

Ears should not be too low set or big and thick. Teeth should be neither undershot nor overshot but the revised standard of the breed allows that a scissor bite is acceptable.

The neck should be clean and muscular and slope into well laid shoulders with forelegs straight and of good bone.

When judging the forequarters the elbow should not be slack or the legs bowed. The dog should stand with his legs well under him, neither narrow in front nor too wide. The body should be short coupled, deep in the brisket and ribs well sprung. The hind-quarters should be strong and muscular with well bent stifle and hocks well let down and not cow hocked. A straight stifle gives a stilted action. The dog should stand well forward on his toes and not sink back on his pasterns which denotes weakness.

The tail should not be gay by which I mean not carried well above the level of the back but in action should be carried level with the spine in a flowing line. It should not be curled at the tip and should be short enough to balance the rest of the body.

The coat can be flat or wavy, well feathered with a dense undercoat. The colour varies considerably from cream to dark golden but should not be white or mahogany. The standard says any shade of gold or cream. There has been a tendency towards very pale cream bordering on white but it is difficult to draw a line on what is definitely outside the standard as dogs tend to darken with each change of coat. Hence puppies may be seen in the ring which look almost white. However, they should be well within the standard when seen two or three years later.

Pigmentation is important and should be black or dark brown on the nose, eye rims, lips, and if very good the nails and pads of the feet will also be black. This is an hereditary feature which should not be overlooked. In very cold weather and particularly if the dog has been working a lot, the black pigmentation sometimes fades temporarily. But although the nose may look pink there is usually some black pigmentation around the edge and it will recover its normal appearance by the spring.

MOVEMENT

Movement is very important and varies considerably. Front action is often bad owing to faulty shoulders. A straight shoulder restricts the movement and causes the animal to plait or pin toe. Others pace like a trotting pony which is equally bad but fortunately not so frequently seen these days as it used to be. The ideal is a good forward stride followed by the hindleg lifted from the hocks and thrust forward with a good driving action. Each forward movement should be straight giving a level easy flow of movement.

Too often one sees the hocks close together and a short stride with the hocks hardly lifted off the ground. In action the hocks should be three to four inches apart neither curving inwards nor outwards. If the dog is made correctly it should not require placing or 'topping and tailing' as it is called. However, it is up to the exhibitor to make the most of his exhibit in the way he chooses.

It is equally bad to see an exhibitor doing practically nothing whatsoever to get the dog to show himself well. Those exhibiting for the first time should watch more experienced breeders or even go to handling classes.

These are getting very much more popular and are usually organised by Obedience Training Societies. They are of great benefit to dog and handler especially if you are going to bring out a new puppy. It gets him used to other dogs and people.

Matches are also a good prep school for the show ring. These are run by Canine Societies usually once a month and make an excellent training ground and social evening. The dogs are brought out in pairs and judged either as a knock out competition or American style where each competitor meets every other competitor. This method takes much longer but it gives the dog much more practice.

To my knowledge we have no professional handlers in Golden Retrievers at present but I think that a more professional attitude could be adopted with benefit. This does not necessarily mean 'Topping and tailing'.

One only has to watch the professional handler to realise how much co-operation they manage to get out of the dog they are handling.

This was brought home to me after watching professional handlers in America, where the biggest proportion of dogs are professionally handled – by ladies as well as men. I can hear the die-hards of the breed shouting me down as I write this but I am firmly of the opinion that they are expert at their job, move their dogs with finesse and take more trouble in presentation than the vast majority of exhibitors over here.

I am not advocating professional handling in the breed, only that we should learn from their experience. I feel sure that the status of dog breeding will never be raised unless we take a more professional attitude ourselves.

There is no reason why the handler, as well as the dog, should not come into the ring as well groomed as possible.

Method of Judging

Judges vary slightly in their method of judging. Some grade the dogs as they proceed. This method means that all the dogs which have been seen have to be kept alert and showing themselves throughout the class and consequently this is very tiring for the first dogs seen in the class.

Other judges discard all the dogs they do not consider good enough immediately they have been handled by the judge. This method is very discouraging for the exhibitors and gives the impression that the exhibitor is not getting a fair deal. Entry fees are high and each exhibitor feels that he is entitled to a second look. This is the easiest method as far as the judge is concerned. By the time he or she has been through all the dogs he has probably more than halved the size of the class and has therefore fewer dogs to concentrate upon.

However, it does cause a considerable amount of discontent amongst the exhibitors and is not a method to be recommended.

The most common method used is the practice of going over each dog individually and at the end picking out eight or ten of the most promising ones and making a final placing from these dogs. This seems the most satisfactory way to me but even so some judges pick their dogs in order of their final placing and never alter their decision once they have called a dog out. I am aways a little sceptical when I see this done because until you have a line up of four or five dogs you cannot judge one against another, particularly if they have been called from opposite ends of the ring.

Golden classes are usually very big ones and it is almost impossible to keep a dog showing all the time, therefore it is best to let him relax after he has been seen.

Show Presentation

This should start several weeks before the show date. Trimming is very important and anyone owning a Golden should learn to do this himself. Many otherwise good dogs get left out of the cards on account of their rough and untidy appearance. The art of good presentation is something which must be learnt by trial and error and no doubt everyone has their own method. I am constantly asked what needs to be done and how to do it. Many owners seem to be frightened to use any instruments on their dog's coat.

I am not advising excessive trimming as this is not generally necessary or for that matter correct but some tidying up does certainly improve the general outline of many exhibits. Some coats need far more attention than others, particularly wavy coats which are the most difficult to control.

Provide yourself with a pair of thinning scissors either serrated on one or both sides, a pair of long-bladed ordinary scissors, a Duplex comb and a steel comb together with a brush and hound glove. These are the first essentials; other types of combs, brushes, scissors and razors can be added to your equipment later on if you wish.

To start with, the ears should be cleaned up as there is generally quite a lot of dead fluffy hair at the base of the ear. This can to some extent be plucked with finger and thumb but a sharp Duplex comb is less painful for the dog. The secret of good trimming is to leave no obvious cut marks. It is most important to thin out the fur around the neck. Lift the ear flaps and with the thinning scissors cut with upward movement to the ear base. If neglected this part will mat and become knotted. It should be kept really short so that the air can get to the inside of the ear which helps to keep it healthy. The front of the neck also needs attention as some Goldens tend to grow quite a ruffle around the neck which quite spoils its outline and generally makes it look as though the neck is shorter than it is. With the thinning scissors continue to cut upwards and thoroughly comb out wherever you have cut. Now with the Duplex comb trim off any loose and straggling hairs. Next turn your attention to the feet and hocks. With your long-bladed scissors cut around the shape of the foot. If the scissors are really sharp you will get a nice neat finish. Do not cut away the hair between the toes except to remove any which are protruding.

Hocks usually have a growth of thick hair at the back which is untidy and can be improved by the use of thinning scissors and comb. If feet are kept well trimmed it is surprising how much less dirt they bring into the house. Now the tail which is very important as this can alter the whole balance of the dog. I have found when judging that here again many people seem timid about trimming the tail and often leave straggling bits at the end.

This is a job which must be done at least a week before the show so that there are no decided cut marks. Take the tail and run your fingers down to the tip of the last vertebra. On measuring this should come down to the level of the hocks. With the thinning scissors cut straight across it several times to thin it out. Comb out and then trim off the remaining hairs with a Duplex comb. Now spread out the tail and shape with the thinning scissors finishing with the Duplex comb to make a neat appearance. Never at any time use ordinary scissors on the coat except on the feet.

To get the best results the feet should be left until the day before the show. If the dog's coat has been allowed to get out of hand do not attempt to do too much at one time. It can become very tedious for the dog to stand

Opposite: Ch. Deerf-lite Endeavour of Yeo and her daughter Caravelle of Yeo. Owned by Mrs Lucille Sawtell.

Below: Ch. Braconcott Alcide. By Ch. Teecon Ambassador ex Amber of Aldercarr. Owned by Mrs C. D. Barclay of Bracondale, Norwich.

for long periods and it is far better to do a little every day. It is also less tiring for the operator to stand the dog on a low table rather than try to do it in a semi-stooping position.

BATHING

I am not of the opinion that a Golden Retriever should be bathed at any time unless it is absolutely necessary. Some coats of great density are definitely best left alone except for the feathering on the hind-quarters and tail which can be shampooed. The object to my mind of bathing should be to clean the coat and not just to fluff it up and make it look pretty on the day of a show. Many judges may be fooled by the added dimensions a freshly bathed dog may appear to have which would present a very different picture if seen between shows. There are parts of the country, mainly in the north and midlands, where coats do get very dirty and in this case bathing before the show does seem justified but it should be done several days before the show so that it has had time to settle down again. I have seen puppies which still have a puppy coat appear in the ring looking like Polar bears with enormous winter coats which have obviously been bathed. I think that it is a highly dangerous operation to bath a puppy in mid-winter or for that matter any dog unless adequate drying arrangements have been made. For a gun dog to go swimming in winter is one thing but to bath it and remove all the natural oils is quite another. In the first place a Golden can swim for long periods and the water never penetrates to its skin because of its undercoat but when it has been bathed its coat is wholly saturated and this is quite a different thing.

Similarly a dog who has shed his winter undercoat is more vulnerable to chills and care should be taken to see that he does not stand about after swimming but should be rubbed down with a chamois leather or towel.

If it is deemed necessary to bath the dog all over then provide yourself with a good hair shampoo and bath rinse or conditioner to put back the oils in the coat to give it a good bloom. All dogs want to have a good shake when they come out of the bath so it is as well to do this where it does not matter. After giving him a good rub down then bring him into the house and let him dry off. If it is a wavy coated dog special care should be given by combing the coat whilst it is drying so that it lies in the correct position and does not curl up.

A hand-operated hair dryer is an excellent thing to have by you to dry your dogs especially in winter time. The sooner they are dried the better and they should not be put back in the kennel still damp particularly in cold weather. If the atmosphere is not too keen outside then a brisk walk or gallop in a field will help to finish off the drying process as long as you do not allow him to roll in any dirt, which is usually the first thing he wants to do to get rid of the scent of shampoo and disguise himself by rolling in manure or other strong smelling matter.

I think that a lot of the illness we hear of following winter shows such as Cruft's and others is brought on by chills after bathing. I am thinking not only of Golden Retrievers but other large breeds which have to be bathed for shows and kennelled out of doors. When dogs live indoors the problem is not so great. I have known a dog completely unable to lift his tail the day after bathing; similarly, swimming has had the same effect.

I have learnt by bitter experience, having arrived at a show the day after bathing even if it has been just the hind-quarters and the tail, to find that the dog could not lift it at all. People have laughed and thought I was joking when I have said that he has got a cold in his tail but this is perfectly true and is a condition known in Labrador circles as 'water tail'. It is a form of fibrositis and is quite painful. The dog looks miserable because he cannot raise his tail. He holds it horizontally for a few inches and then it hangs down in a vertical droop.

SHOWING

You will need some of your equipment at the show so pack a small bag the night before with all the necessary articles in it such as a brush, comb and a bowl for water. If you have room it is a good idea to take a bottle of water with you as this saves time looking for a tap or tank of water on arrival at the show. A chamois leather is useful in case the dog gets wet or dirty walking from the car to his bench. You will need a collar and chain to tether him to his show bench if it is a benched show. And of course you must remember your show lead and titbits to tempt him in the ring. These are best kept in a polythene bag or in your pocket. After buying a catalogue find out exactly in which ring you are being judged and at approximately what time. So often novices miss their classes through ignorance of show procedure. See that your dog has been well exercised before leaving home and allow enough time *en route* for him to relieve himself and again before going into the ring. It is not permitted to take a dog off the bench for more than fifteen minutes at a time.

When the time comes for your breed to be judged collect your ring number from the ring steward as you enter the ring and be sure that you have a pin, brooch or club badge to which it can be attached. It is usual for the judge to ask all exhibitors to run their dogs around the ring together. This helps to loosen up the dogs and gives the judge some idea of the quality of the class he has to judge. Sometimes one or two are quite eye catching and move extremely well whilst others do not impress and are sluggish in their movement.

When your turn comes for your puppy to be gone over by the judge it is up to you to make the most of him and this is where your previous training will count. When asked to move him make sure whether the judge wants you to go straight up the ring and back or as some judges do in a triangle. If

Sh. Ch. Brensham Audacity. Best of Breed at Cruft's 1979. By Ch. Stolford Happy Lad ex Moonswell Dora of Brensham. Owned by Mrs Wood.

you watch the previous exhibits you will know. It is very annoying for the judge if the exhibitor does not pay attention and goes in the wrong direction and wastes a lot of valuable time especially when there is a big entry to be judged. Whether going or coming back to the judge do try to do so in a straight line. Do not let the dog pull from side to side and do not jerk the lead too violently as this may make the dog plait in front, which in normal circumstances he may not do.

By plaiting I mean passing one foot in front of the other as one would do if plaiting string. Always keep your eye on the judge and see that your puppy looks his best at the moment he comes back to look at him. It is not wise to keep him on his toes all the time. If it is a big class he will tend to lose interest. Try to command his attention immediately the last dog has been seen and do not crowd your fellow exhibitors on either side of you. Some dogs are 'Creepers'. By this I mean that they are apt to edge forward whilst you are showing them. This is an annoying habit and you will not be at all popular with your neighbour as gradually, and very often unwittingly, you will block his dog from being seen by the judge; in a crowded ring this is easily done.

Win or lose never let this become of such importance to you that you cannot take the verdict sportingly. Very often the dog who is continually placed second or third is the one who in the end will win through to greater honours. One must not be disheartened. If the dog is good it will make the grade one day.

Nord. and Finnish Champion Deerflite Salome owned by M. Ericson and U–B Karlmann, Stockholm. Sired by Sh. Ch. Concord of Yeo ex Deerflite Pheasant. Bred by Mrs Borrow.

Cruft's

To win at Cruft's is a dream shared by many owners of promising dogs. Even to qualify for entry is a distinction for all dogs except Champions must have won awards in specified classes at Championship Shows held the previous year. Judging takes place each day in about thirty rings and there may be more than nine thousand dogs in all. Excitement builds up as the Best of Breed winners compete against each other, and from the winners in each group the Supreme Champion is chosen. There are also classes for Obedience leading to the title of Supreme Obedience Champion.

Although there is great prestige in winning at Cruft's, competition within a breed can be keener in Breed Club Championship Shows where entry is not restricted. Some of the dogs which have qualified for Cruft's may not attend because they are out of coat or for maternal and other reasons.

However, Cruft's is a unique social occasion. The Show is open to the general public and crowds are large. Many visitors come from abroad to buy dogs and to watch the judging; much business is done around the rings and in the various bars. After the winter period of few big shows, breeders and exhibitors find it pleasant to meet again in February, compare notes, discuss the merits of dogs which have come to the fore in the past year, and plan future litters.

5 The Standard of the Breed

The Standard for the Golden Retriever

(Reproduced by courtesy of the Kennel Club)

General Appearance: Symmetrical, balanced, active, powerful, level mover; sound with kindly expression.

Characteristics: Biddable, intelligent and possessing natural working ability.

Temperament: Kindly, friendly and confident.

Head and Skull: Balanced and well chiselled, skull broad without coarseness; well set on neck, muzzle powerful, wide and deep. Length of foreface approximately equals length from well-defined stop to occiput. Nose black.

Eyes: Dark brown, set well apart, dark rims.

Ears: Moderate size, set on approximate level with eyes.

Mouth: Jaws strong, with a perfect, regular and complete scissor bite, i.e. upper teeth closely overlapping lower teeth and set to the jaws.

Neck: Good length, clean and muscular.

Forequarters: Forelegs straight with good bone, shoulders well laid back, long in blade with upper arm of equal length placing legs well under body. Elbows close fitting.

Body: Balanced, short coupled, deep through heart. Ribs deep, well sprung. Level topline.

Hindquarters: Loin and legs strong and muscular, good second thighs, well bent stifles. Hocks well let down, straight when viewed from rear, neither turning in nor out. Cow hocks highly undesirable.

Feet: Round and cat-like.

Tail: Set on and carried level with back, reaching to hocks, without curl at top.

Gait/Movement: Powerful with good drive. Straight and true in front and rear. Stride long and free with no sign of hackney action in front.

Coat: Flat or wavy with good feathering, dense water resisting undercoat.

Colour: Any shade of gold or cream, neither red nor mahogany. A few white hairs on chest only permissible.

Size: Height at withers; Dogs 56-61 cm (22-24 ins); Bitches 51-56 cm (20-22 ins).

Faults: Any departure from the foregoing points should be considered a fault and the seriousness with which the fault should be regarded should be in exact proportion to its degree.

Note: Male animals should have two apparently normal testicles fully descended into the scrotum.

2 Topography

1	occiput	12	point of shoulder	22	flank
2	frontal bones	13	forechest	23	loin
3	stop	14	brisket	24	thigh
4	flews	15	upper arm	25	hock joint
5	cheek	15a	elbow	26	point of hock
6	crest of neck	16	forearm	27	rear pastern
7	withers	17	knee	28	second thigh
8	back	18	front pastern	29	feathering
9	croup	19	ribs	30	ruff
10	tail	20	tuckup	31	muzzle
11	shoulder	21	stifle		

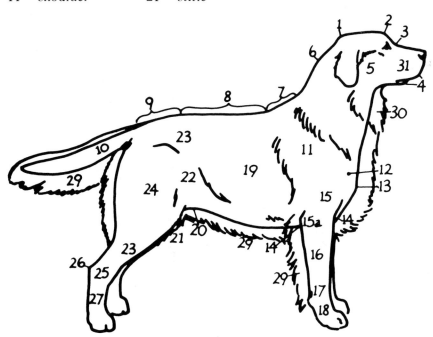

Miss Marcia Schlehr of Michigan, U.S.A. has skilfully illustrated and commented on the conformation and physical structure of the Golden Retriever in the following pages. Her diagrams and short comments set out to instruct most ably where words alone would fail and I am greatly indebted to her for allowing me to include them in this book. I feel that all who love the breed and are anxious to learn more about it will profit from a study of the pages that follow.

Topography *Continued*

A1 height
B1 length
C1 slope of pelvis
D1D2 line of femur
 (thigh)
D2D3 line of tibia
 (second thigh)
D3D4 line of metacarpus
 (hock); rear pastern
D1D2D3D4 rear angulation
 (hindquarters)

E1E2 line of scapula
 (shoulder)
E2D3 line of humerus
 (upper arm)
E3E4 line of radius & ulna
 (forearm)
E4E5 slope of pastern
 or metacarpals
E1E2E3E4 front angulation
 (forequarters)
F1 backline

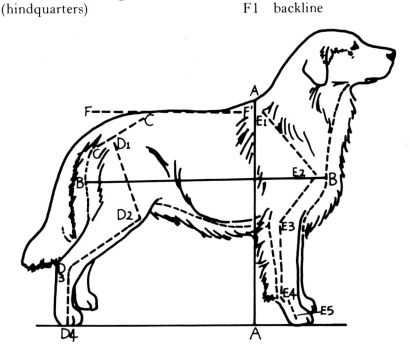

3   Head and Head Faults

(a) Prominent occiput and frontal bones giving bumpy skull. Roman nose – convex line between stop and tip of nose instead of straight profile. Nose too pointed and projecting. Ears large, low-set; neck throaty.

(b) 'Wet' head; overdeveloped flews, skin wrinkles on skull. Ears large but well-carried here when dog is at attention. Good skull and stop, but too coarse throughout.

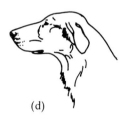

(c) Inadequate skull for long muzzle. Eyes too open and large in appearance with droopy 'houndy' lids, poor Spaniel-like expression. Ears too large, long, and curling like a hound's. Missing premolar at 'x'.

(d) A common sort of head, lacking in major faults and also lacking outstanding good points. Skull is flat and weak; no stop; nose too projecting (shark-face). Ears small and well-carried, here in repose. Good neck and throat.

(e) Too round in skull; cheeky; muzzle snipey, and doesn't fit well on to skull. Nose lacking pigment (Dudley nose). Eyes too small and slanting, giving 'oriental' expression. Eye rims too light. Thin, stiff, 'flyaway' ears.

(f) Dish-faced (concave line between stop and tip of nose). Stop too pronounced. Eyes pale in colour, giving 'hard' untypical expression. Lower jaw seems to project beyond upper; this dog is very likely undershot.

4 Bite

(a) Scissors bite. Desired as strongest and least wearing. The inner surfaces of the upper incisors contact the outer surfaces of the lowers. There is a relatively tight meshing of the incisors and canines (eyeteeth). The small premolars do not touch; this is 'carrying space'.

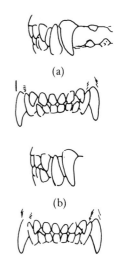

(b) Even, level, or pincers bite. The direct edge-to-edge meeting of the incisors is quite wearing. Usually only the centre two pairs will so touch: it is normal in both scissors and level bites for the third pair (nearest the eyeteeth) of uppers to have a slightly wider-set, outward-turning position somewhat resembling the eye-tooth.
It is not uncommon for the centremost two lower incisors, and occasionally others, to be slightly out of line with their neighbours. Such minor irregularities should not be unduly penalised.

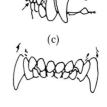

(c) Overshot. The incisors of the upper jaw overlap and fail to contact the incisors of the lower jaw. 'Pig jaw.' There is often a noticeable space at 'x'.

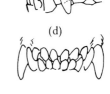

(d) Undershot. A forward set or extra length of lower jaw causes the incisors of the lower jaw to overlap or project beyond the incisors of the upper jaw when the mouth is closed. Generally there is a more or less considerable space at 'x'.
In both undershot and overshot jaws the condition is the result of an abnormal relationship of the upper jaw to the lower (or vice versa). The discrepancy is often noticeable in the incorrect meshing of molars and premolars as well.

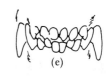

(e) Misalignment of teeth of lower jaw. Central incisors markedly out of line, forward of the rest of the lower teeth. This in itself does not constitute undershot bite. Undershot or overshot mouths may or may not have misaligned teeth.

(f) Extremely undershot mouth. The lower canine should occupy the space 'x' but the lower jaw is set too far forward. Such a dog will have difficulty in eating, and bitches hampered in caring for puppies.

5   Body Structure and Rib Cage

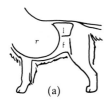

(a) The thoracic area enclosed by the rib cage must be capacious to provide maximum volume for heart and lungs, shaped to allow for efficient use of forelegs and proper attachment of muscular systems. Posterior to the rib cage, the loin area consists of very strong muscles of the spinal 'bridge' connecting front and rear, and the abdominal area containing many vital organs.

The rib cage (r) is both deep and long, with prominent forechest, depth at brisket, and depth at the rear part ('ribs carried well back'). The loin (l) is comparatively short from rib to hip, deep, wide when seen from top, with heavy musculature. The flank (f) is deep with a slight tuckup and strong muscular abdomen. The loin is very slightly arched due to the spine's natural curve of support in this area, but because of the strong muscling over ribs and spine, the backline maintains a level profile.

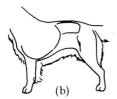

(b) This dog has adequate depth at the elbow, but compared to (a) is decidedly lacking in depth at the last ribs ('herring gutted') giving much less internal capacity. He is too 'cut up in the flank', with a rather long loin (long-coupled), too much arched, giving a rangey, racey look. This dog is actually the same height and length overall as both (a) and (c).

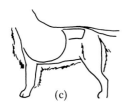

(c) This dog gives an appearance of great length, due to a foreleg assembly set far forward on a short rib cage (forechest has disappeared); loin is long, lacking strength and firmness. These factors result in a slack, soft backline. The lack of proper muscle tone is also evident in the soft, paunchy abdomen. Such weaknesses in mid-section prevent efficient transmission of power from hindquarters and contribute to fatigue and susceptibility to injury.

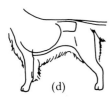

(d) The 'shelly' body. Shallow in depth, lacking in development throughout. Absence of forechest is disguised somewhat by forequarter angulation. Do not be misled by abundant coat; this weedy sort lacks greatly in working qualities.

(e) Diagrammatic cross-sections of rib cage shows good spring of rib arching out from vertebrae, then dropping in a deep oval to sternum, allowing both adequate internal volume for lung and heart, and easy movement of forelegs alongside rib cage. The curve of rib and angle with spine allow ribs to rotate out and forward to position shown by dotted lines, increasing volume as necessary with exertion.

(f) 'Barrel-ribbed'. May be equally as capacious as (e), but lacking the ability to increase volume as does (e). The very wide ribs will cause difficulty in smooth movement of forelegs, resulting in awkwardness moving or swimming.

(f)

(g) Flatsided and lacking spring of rib. Internal capacity is severely limited. Those 'speed' breeds which ask for narrowness of chest still require good spring at the top, and very deep, long ribs well carried back, providing adequate capacity (they are also much lighter in weight, with long, fine but strong, bones and efficient structure for their purpose of speed). This dog will lack buoyancy and stability in swimming, compared to (e).

(g)

6   Forequarters

Note the straight vertical column of bones from the point of the shoulder (x) down to the footpads for most efficiency in movement. The ribs are well-sprung from the spine, then drop with moderate curve, allowing easy movement of the leg assembly beside the rib cage.

The shoulder blades (scapulae) lie snugly upon the rib cage. Their placement can be properly determined only by examination with the hands; they should be long, fairly close together at the withers, and from the side, the central ridge or spine of the scapula slopes at an angle close to 45 degrees from the vertical.

The 'bone' of the forelegs should be straight and sturdy, never fine, thin or delicate, nor should it be heavy, round and coarse like a draft-horse's. Muscling should be well-developed throughout, but a bulging, 'loaded' appearance of the shoulder is not desired.

The well-developed chest affords great heart and lung capacity for endurance, and buoyancy and stability when swimming. Deepest part of the chest reaches easily to the level of the elbows; the sternum or 'keel-bone' comes well forward in front to help form a full forechest, thus providing for even more volume within the rib cage and also anchorage for various muscles of neck and forequarters.

Due to the Golden's dense coat and featherings, all visual examination should be verified when possible by thorough examination with the hands; the position, form, and quality of bone structure, muscle, and coat can be accurately determined only in this way.

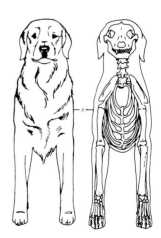

Forequarters *continued*

(a) Front too wide, feet turned in. Such a dog will move clumsily. He may or may not be 'out at elbows', but when moving will give that impression. Often a too-round rib cage (barrel-bodied) will result in such a front, or it may be due to an actual bowing of the forelegs.

(b) 'French-front' or 'fiddle front'. Loose shoulders and turned out feet. May be caused by inherently weak or poor structure, or broken down by activity such as excessive jumping before full growth.

(c) Far too narrow, lacking remarkably in both depth and width of chest. Due to the excessive lack of chest the elbows are held too close ('tied in') turning the feet outward and resulting in an 'east and west' front quite different from (b)'s.

(d) A good front. There is a very slight sideways sloping of the pasterns – but the feet point straight ahead and are not turned. When the feet converge in gaiting, the pasterns will become vertical, letting the foot contact the ground squarely rather than on the outer edge as is often the case with a 'dead straight' front.

(e) Angle view of out-at-elbows front, with turned-in feet. Incorrect shoulder/elbow assembly permits this turned set of foreleg with loose shoulders. Improper muscle development attempting to compensate for this looseness often results in 'loaded' shoulders (bunchy, bulging muscle).

7 Hind-quarters

In the rear as in the front, note the straight line of bones from hip joint to foot pad, allowing most efficient transmission of power in movement. Because the rear limbs supply the drive and 'push' they are particularly important. Except in swimming, when they provide a major motive force, the forelimbs serve primarily for support and absorption of impact. A dog may be able to make some compensation for inefficient forequarter structure, but if the rear is bad the dog simply 'hasn't got it' and no excellence in front can supply that thrust and power.

This dog is posed as in the show ring, with the rear spread slightly wider than the front. A dog standing naturally would place the feet on a line almost directly beneath the hip joints for a more natural balance with less tension.

A wide pelvis provides for better development and attachment of musculature. The rear can scarcely be over-muscled; it should never seem weak or too small for the front assembly. Hind feet are slightly smaller in diameter than the front feet, which take more in the way of impact and weight-carrying.

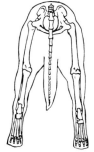

The tail reaches to the hock joint in bone. It is the dog's 'rudder' and balancing device, as well as indicator of emotion, and should be quite heavily muscled, particularly at the base. A somewhat short, thick tail is preferable to a whiplike or long one. It should hang straight or slightly curved when at rest, and be very densely coated overall, with a thick rather rounded appearance, not a setter-like thin flag.

(a) This rear is undesirable because of the lack of muscle development, which may be only a result of poor condition, or may not. If so it is probably to be preferred over the others shown here. The tail is too short, however.

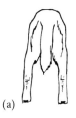

(a)

(b) Out at the stifles. The straight line from hip to foot is lost. This is not quite the same as cowhocks since the rear pasterns are parallel, even though the toes turn out.

(b)

(c) Cowhocks. A common expression of weakness of the rear assembly, either inherited or environmental. Such a dog cannot move well. Some cowhocked dogs may be better in stifle than this, but convergence of the hock and splay of the rear pasterns is a severe fault. Poor tail.

(c)

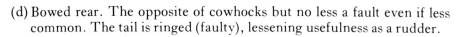

Hind-quarters *continued*

(d) Bowed rear. The opposite of cowhocks but no less a fault even if less common. The tail is ringed (faulty), lessening usefulness as a rudder.

(e) A rear which may, at first, appear to be acceptable, but there is some reason why this dog is favouring the right leg. This may be temporary, such as a cut pad or minor sprain, or might be an indication of some inherent defect such as a faulty hip joint, slipped stifle, etc. Look well about him if this is a consistent feature and not just the result of off-balance posing.

8   Shoulder Placement

(a) Ideal forequarter assembly. The 45-degree layback of shoulder blade and its 90-degree angle with the humerus allows for greatest length of reach in movement, best muscular development of shoulder assembly and, with slightly sloping pastern, greatest shock absorbency. With the point of support (foot pads) directly beneath the shoulder blades this front is well-balanced, ready for action, but at ease. Note the strong neck running well back and strongly united with the back and shoulders.

(b) Poorly angulated forequarter, with short upright scapulae limiting stride; their forward position forces the blades far apart at the withers and weakens what should be a strong smooth merging of neck into shoulders and back.

(c) 'Wolf shoulder'. Longer blade than (b) and better angulation, but wrongly set. The shoulder is too nearly vertical, the upper arm angling too far beneath the body. Sometimes such a dog may appear to move well, by excess motion of the shoulder blade to create some length of stride.

(d) 'Terrier front'. The blade is of fair length and well laid back, but the upper arm is much too vertical and pastern is too upright and rigid. Such a dog may lift the forefeet quite high in order to get sufficient stride, but it is wasted motion. Many setters have this type of front, with exaggerated front action.

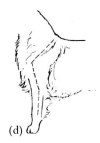

(d)

9   Desirable Rear

(a) Desirable rear. Proper angulation throughout allows for greatest length of thigh and second thigh and long strong muscles for optimum reach and power with endurance.

(a)

(b) A too-steeply sloping croup makes the dog 'stand under'. This dog cannot extend his leg backward properly for 'push' and follow-through. Short second thigh and lack of angulation at the hock limit stride and leverage.

(b)

(c) Over-angulated rear. It is practically impossible to get musculature to support such extreme angulation in a breed the weight of a retriever. The angled-under rear pasterns ('sickle hocks') do not straighten when moving and any advantage gained by the extreme angle is lost.

(c)

(d) This might be an acceptable rear except that the hock, being already extended (straight-angled), cannot extend further for a powerful push. Don't be fooled by snappy flexion on the forward reach; 'push' comes only when the foot is on the ground. Straight hocks are generally accompanied by short second thighs.

(d)

(e) Too-straight rear, lacking any proper angulation. Also too-flat pelvis. Although the leg appears longer than (a), the bones are shorter. Since this leg cannot extend much further when moving, the dog may show great height in action but little length of stride unless he lowers his body closer to the ground to create angulation. Either way he must exert more effort to cover the same distance as (a). The flat pelvis sets the tail too high for best use in swimming or running, when it should stay low for balance.

(e)

10   Front Movement

(a) Proper front, moving. The straight column of bones from foot to point of shoulder provides most efficient transmission of power. The feet converge in order to stay under the centreline of gravity, but never interfere with each other. The faster the trot, the more the feet will converge. A dog is single tracking when the feet are set down directly ahead of one another on the line of travel. This is NOT a fault – unless the dog is interfering. Because of the well developed chest a retriever should not be expected to move as smoothly in front as some other breeds; but he must move easily and efficiently. (Singletracking as a result of some structural fault is of course undesirable.)

(b) Too wide. Dog will tend to 'roll' as weight shifts slightly from side to side trying to stay over the point of support.

(c) Bowed front. Feet turn inwards. Dog will probably tire easily and be subject to injury due to unnatural stress upon the leg.

(d) Too narrow. This dog may move very smoothly and look quite good from the side, because he has no chest to limit his front action. This lack of chest is highly undesirable.

(e) Paddling or winging. The feet are thrown sideways as they are brought forward, denoting some weakness in shoulder/elbow assembly.

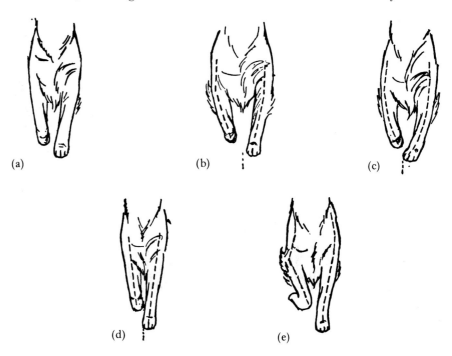

(a)   (b)   (c)

(d)   (e)

11   Rear Movement

(a) Desirable rear, moving at the trot. As the feet converge with increased speed the straight line from hip to foot is maintained. Convergence allows the dog to more easily keep his centre of gravity over the line of travel (i.e., over the point of support, the foot).

(b) Bowed rear. Wasted power due to curved line of transmission. Subjects leg and foot to undue stress; note weight on outer side of foot.

(c) Cow hocks. May be due to faulty structure or to muscular weakness. The dog tracks wide yet his hocks interfere. Attempting to avoid interference, he will throw his legs sideways to swing around the opposite leg, wasting power.

(d) Moving too close. Tracking this closely with the rear pasterns parallel, there is bound to be interference as the feet pass each other, unless they are swung sideways, or raised very high on the forward step to clear.

(e) Even though this dog is 'crossing over', there may be little interference because as the left foot is raised for the forward reach, still maintaining the straight line from hip to foot, it can clear the right foot without sideways swing. However, the dog which crosses over is far too liable to interfere, especially on any irregular surface. Very seldom is the proper straight line (plane) maintained as in this dog. Bow-legged dogs often cross over.

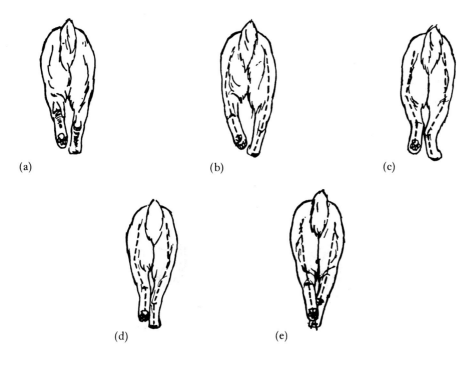

(a)   (b)   (c)

(d)   (e)

12   Gait

Here is a good moving dog, plenty of reach and a powerful drive of hind-quarters. His gait looks effortless and graceful. A minimum of exertion is needed to gain fullest advantage of his most efficient structure. Let's follow him through the cycle of one stride in 'slow motion'.

(a) Here he is supported on the left diagonal pair of legs, just having raised the opposite (right) diagonal to begin a new stride. Note his easy, confident air, level backline, well-carried head and tail.

(b) The body of the dog is being carried forward over the supporting diagonal by the inertia of the thrust just ended; the non-supporting pair of legs is collected and brought forward. They are raised only enough to clear the ground sufficiently, with no useless 'hackney' height of action.

(c) Now the supporting legs begin the powerful push or drive of propulsion. This is the moment of greatest collection. Until now the dog has been moving forward on the 'left-over' push of the previous stride; now he begins a new thrust.

As in (b) you can note that the cycle of the foreleg's movement is a small fraction ahead of that of the rear in timing. The reason for this will be apparent a bit later.

(d) The non-supporting (right) diagonal begins its reach for a new stride. They are far advanced of the supporting legs, but have not yet reached full extension. The supporting legs are thrusting powerfully, gripping the ground strongly with the toes. Level backline indicates good transmission of thrust from the rear through the back to the fore part of the body without unnecessary sway or bobbing.

(e) Period of greatest extension. The fully extended right diagonal is just about to contact the ground; the left has finished its thrust with a powerful sweeping follow-through. At full speed of the trot the best-moving dogs will actually have an instant's suspension when none of the feet are contacting the ground.

Note the great length of stride made possible by the long-boned, properly angulated limbs, and the 'opening up' of the shoulder and stifle assemblies.

Now we can see why the forefoot's time is that fraction ahead of the rear foot's: here the forefoot has left the ground in time for the rear foot of the same side to land on the same line or track without striking the forefoot. Without this timing the dog would have three alternatives in order to avoid hitting his forefeet: move the rear feet to the side (sidetracking or crabbing), move wide behind, or else considerably shorten stride. It is for this reason that racing trotting horses wear protective quarter-boots on their front pasterns.

The next phase of the stride would be identical to (a) except on the opposite diagonal.

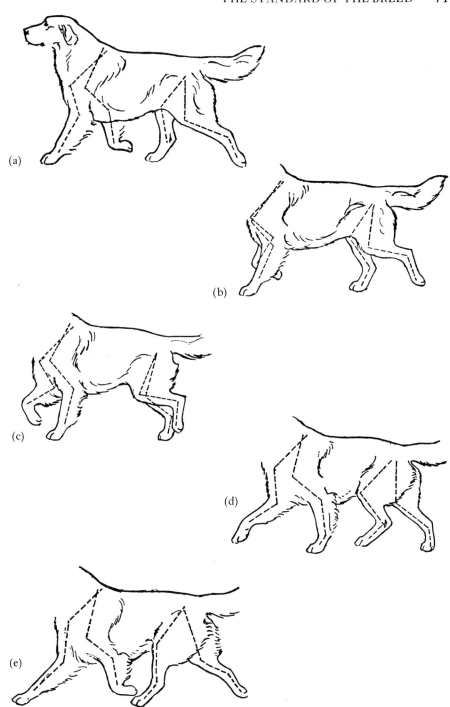

(a)

(b)

(c)

(d)

(e)

13   Feet

(a) Desirable forefoot. Deep thick pads for sturdiness, nails short and strong, toes well arched and held compactly together for endurance and strength. The slightly sloped pastern allows for 'spring' and shock-absorbence, as the front feet take the larger part of impact and weight-carrying. Medium size. Tiny feet indicate unwanted fineness and less support area; oversize feet may be so because splayed, or due to coarse and clumsy bone.

(b) Open, splayed foot, thin pads, weak pastern. Such a foot 'gives' too much with impact and is much more susceptible to injury than a tight foot, as well as being less strong and less efficient.

(c) Terrier foot. Ultra-tight with vertical pastern, has no 'give' to it and does not absorb shock, but transmits it to the higher parts of the leg. All right for terriers, but not for the comparatively heavy retriever.

(d) The terrier foot which has knuckled over in the pastern. This is definitely not a strong or enduring foot, since each impact will tend to force the knee farther over; it is extremely difficult to maintain stability in such a case.

(e) Hindfoot is slightly narrower than the forefoot, but still with well-arched, tight toes and good pads. Rear pastern (metatarsals) should be fairly short, and perpendicular to ground when standing. Position of rear dew-claws is indicated at (dc). Very rare in Goldens, and very faulty, as they interfere greatly with proper movement and are easily subject to injury.

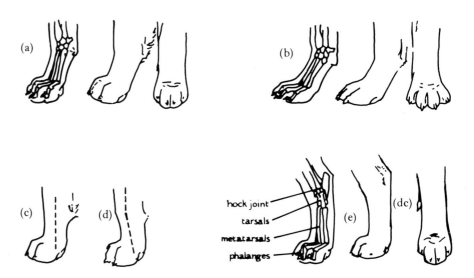

6 Breeding

A breeding kennel can take several forms and it is unfortunate that one only has to mention the word 'dog breeder' to the average person to be regarded as someone rather peculiar or having some kind of kink. Most people have not the slightest idea of what goes into breeding good dogs and imagine all dog shows to be like the ones they see held at the local village fête. They do not realise the years one has spent building up a strain, all the hard work, the disappointments and sometimes sheer bad luck which have gone before, to enable one to produce good and successful dogs conforming as nearly as possible to the standard of the breed.

No hobby could possibly help one make so many friends throughout the whole country and in many cases all over the world. Interest in dogs can take many forms and I have seen people who have been shy and retiring blossom out into confident, eager and active people with a challenge in life which has knocked years off their age. One can put as much or as little into it according to the time available. There are so many facets to the hobby and surely the Golden Retriever is one of the most versatile breeds to own.

Apart from showing and breeding one can attend gundog training classes and working tests and field trials. In these days there are obedience classes held in most towns and obedience tests run in conjunction with almost all shows. The Golden Retriever is particularly suitable as a Guide Dog for the Blind and this Association runs a puppy walking scheme for people who are willing to take a puppy and rear it in their home until it is about twelve months old, and old enough to train as a Guide Dog. There are also many social events such as matches, 'teach ins', demonstrations, film shows etc; club dinners, lunches and balls are also a feature of some societies.

It is evident that the dog breeding fraternity have much to be proud of and it is disturbing to them to be confused by the public with the money-grasping puppy farmers who have brought breeding into disrepute.

In recent years the rush to sell dogs abroad for high prices has encouraged people with no knowledge to breed indiscriminately in order to cash in on the overseas market by selling to 'puppy palaces' and very often a life of misery. It is well known that in many countries these puppies are only required as machines to supply an unlimited quantity of puppies for research. In Japan they have no humane way of destroying dogs and there is no society to look after their welfare. It is quite appalling to think of all the horror these innocent animals may have to suffer.

I have seen boxes of young puppies not much more than six weeks old arriving at London airport after an all night journey from remote parts of the country, to be dumped early in the morning at the airline cargo departments, sick and miserable, awaiting dispatch to Tokyo. Without food or water they are sent on their long journey to the fate which lies before them.

The puppy palaces of America are run mainly for the pet market and they offer tempting prices. No doubt some of the inmates do find good homes but I fear that many end up at the hospitals for research if they do not sell at an early age. Nor are we in Britain beyond reproach as there are many dealers here who buy up whole litters from people who find it difficult to sell their puppies or from those who breed solely to supply this type of market. These people care little for the breed nor have they any knowledge of conformation or genetics. Their main object is to acquire a cheap bitch and breed as many litters as possible from her. This type of person should not be confused with the serious dog fancier who has the love of the breed at heart.

It is an expensive business to maintain a kennel of high class stock, and in order to do so the sale of surplus puppies is essential.

Few Golden Retriever breeders keep a large kennel and I would say that ten or twelve is an average number. Of these some will be old age pensioners which most breeders will cherish to the end. Only the commercial kennel would think of putting an old dog down unnecessarily. Many people only breed a litter after much careful thought and when they want to keep a puppy for themselves, and not just for the sake of breeding.

It is necessary to take an impartial look at one's own bitch and observe her faults and failings before choosing a mate for her. Apart from her conformation, temperament must be taken into account. This is generally hereditary although environment plays a big part. A highly strung and nervous person often has a dog of similar temperament but should it change hands this frequently alters completely.

The Stud Dog

It is surprising how often I receive letters and phone calls from the owners of pet dogs offering them to me to use at stud. They assure me that they are beautiful animals and that it is a pity for them not to sire a litter, but they do not know how to set about it.

In these circumstances my answer is generally the same. If the dog is as good as the owner thinks it is then he should show it and prove that it is worthy to sire litters or else he should buy a bitch of his own. It is the prerogative of the bitch's owner to choose which dog he will use and not for the owner of the dog to solicit bitches.

Serious breeders go to a lot of expense and spend a lot of time and thought in breeding a stud dog, and after rearing him well and showing him successfully they will have his eyes tested for hereditary eye diseases and his hips X-rayed for hip dysplasia. Much consideration will have gone into his breeding to be sure that his forebears were as free as possible from these diseases as well as dominant faults that are likely to crop up again, such as light eyes, straight shoulders or gay tail.

It is obvious that none of these things will have been gone into by the pet dog's owner, and for this reason no one should take the line of least resistance and use the dog next door because it is so handy or because the two dogs know each other.

If it means travelling a long way to use the dog most suitable for your bitch do not hesitate to do so. The resulting puppies if well-reared will more than compensate you for the long distance travelled. There are so many well known reliable dogs at stud that no one should use a dog without a reputation.

One dog was brought to me of eight years old. The owner told me that he had such a remarkable temperament that he wanted it perpetuated.

He seemed surprised when I told him that most Goldens did have good temperaments. After going over the dog I found that he had one of the worst undershot mouths I have ever seen. The owner had no idea how serious a fault this was. I also told him that at eight years old it was almost certain that the dog would not have any idea how to mate a bitch if he had never been used before, and probably would not have any inclination to do so.

It sometimes happens that the dog who produces the best progeny is not the one who does the most winning and the discerning breeder will be quick to realise this. The dog in fact who may be considered 'overdone' by most judges, that is to say he may be too strong in head or too heavily boned, may be just the dog to suit some bitches provided his background breeding is correct. He may be a dog who does not show well but in fact has excellent conformation.

The owner of a successful young dog should not rush into using him too soon or too often.

It is advisable, however, to let him have one bitch to mate by the time he is twelve to fifteen months old and then two or three by the time he is eighteen months old. If possible, his first bitch should be a quiet one who has already had a litter. It is important that he should not be put off by a bitch who is likely to turn on him. I think it is a good plan to get him used to mating bitches in the same place every time to start with, such as a garage or large kennel so that he associates the place with the job in hand. Later on when he is more experienced this will not matter and he will be happy to oblige anywhere at any time. Try to avoid feeding him for about two hours before servicing a bitch or he will almost certainly be sick during the procedure.

Two stud dogs kept together need very careful handling and should never be given the opportunity to become jealous of each other. If kennelled together they should not be parted for any length of time as it will not be easy to get them to live happily together again once this has happened. It is important that the stud dog should be kept in the pink of health and condition. His diet should contain plenty of raw meat and I recommend a raw egg and milk daily. Stud dogs are apt to go off their food when there are bitches in season and will lose condition rapidly if not watched. If he has been well cared for throughout his life there is no reason why he should not continue to sire litters at the age of eleven or twelve but it is a wise precaution to mate the dog of this age to a young bitch who is likely to be very fertile.

The Brood Bitch

If you have decided that you wish to breed from your bitch be sure that she is physically mature enough to do so. As a rule the third season is early enough but in some cases when a bitch is late having her first season she may be eighteen months old or more before she comes in season again and in this case you would be justified in breeding from her. Having a litter generally improves a bitch in that she becomes more mature. But to my mind it is hardly fair to expect her to produce a strong and healthy litter when she herself has not had time to develop. So do not rush into mating her if she is small or immature. What is correct for one breed is definitely not correct for another, as some breeds need to be bred from on either their first or second season so do not listen to hearsay as it is not possible to generalise. I constantly have people wanting to bring bitches to be mated and on enquiry find that they are far too young. Usually I find that they have been misinformed by a friend who has a small breed or a farmer who has Russell Terriers and sees no harm in breeding from them every season. If your bitch gives you three to four good litters in her lifetime you will have nothing to complain about, especially if they are large litters and she has reared them well. If for any reason the litter is very small or several die then she may be bred from on the next heat but she must be given a good rest afterwards before breeding from her again, and certainly do not do so if she has experienced a lot of trouble whelping.

Some people go on breeding from their bitches until they are eight, nine and ten years of age, but I doubt if the puppies are as strong and healthy as those bred from a bitch in her prime. To lose a bitch in whelp at this age would to my mind be criminal and yet it does happen.

As a rule Golden Retrievers whelp quite easily but as they get older the greater the strain upon them and the more likely they are to have uterine inertia during whelping which means that the uterus does not contract to expel the whelp. (See 'Whelping')

The Season and Mating Procedure

As soon as the bitch shows any signs of colouring, ring up the owner of the stud dog you have chosen for her and make an appointment to take the bitch to the dog.

It is very important to be accurate about the date of the onset of the season. You should know from the date of her previous one when to expect it, but if in any doubt, take a piece of cotton wool and dab the vulva each morning before she goes out. You will then make no mistake about the right date. Actually with Goldens it is usually quite obvious, but in some breeds it is not so easy to see and if the discharge is very slight the above mentioned method is a most useful one. The vulva itself will become noticeably enlarged, and if a dog is kept he will show a marked interest in the bitch several days before the season starts.

Bitches are usually very regular in the onset of their seasons and once a pattern has been established they continue to come in season accordingly for the rest of their lives. Some have a season every six months, some every seven or eight months, and occasionally one hears of bitches only coming in season once a year.

In these days it is possible to prevent bitches coming in season at all by an injection about a month before the season is due. In the case of a pet bitch this has definite advantages, but if it is intended that the bitch should be bred from at a later date, she must be allowed to have one normal season before the one when she is to be mated.

Another method of prevention is by spaying, which is the removal of the bitch's ovaries. There are varying opinions about the best age at which this should be done. Some vets recommend that bitches should have their first season before the operation, otherwise they tend to run to fat. Personally I do not advise spaying unless the circumstances are exceptional, and it means of course that the bitch can never be bred from, or shown unless she has already had a litter which has been registered.

Some people make a lot of fuss about a bitch coming in season, but where a pet is concerned I can see no difficulty at all. It is only the careless individual who opens the door and lets her out, or leaves her loose in the garden unaccompanied. The usual excuse is that people are too busy, but in fact it takes very little time just to go out with the bitch while she relieves herself, morning, afternoon and evening. She does not need to be constantly taken out. During her season she can be restricted from lying about on carpets, and can be kept in her bed in a room where the floor can be easily cleaned. Most bitches are scrupulously clean in their habits and are seen constantly washing themselves at this time. If you are troubled with stray dogs visiting you, make a point of giving the bitch her exercise away from the locality if possible, by taking her in the car to a field. Some preparation such as Anti-Mate or Keep-Away can be used, but care is still needed as some dogs seem to get wise to the scent.

The duration of the season is usually twenty-one days, but for the first week the bitch is not generally bothered by the attentions of the dog. Although mildly interested he will not attempt to mount her, and she is likely to discourage any advances he makes. However, there are exceptions to every rule, and I would not recommend that she be left unattended with dogs at this time. I have heard of bitches being mated on their third or fourth day.

From the tenth to the fifteenth day the bitch is at the height of her season and it is during this period that she will be willing to stand for a dog. By this time also the vulva will have enlarged and the discharge will have lessened and be paler in colour. I like to mate bitches on the twelfth or thirteenth day.

Before travelling a long distance to the chosen dog it is as well to try the bitch out if you have another dog available to see if she will stand. She will indicate this by curling her tail to one side when approached from the rear by the dog, inviting him to mount her. Alternatively, a hand placed firmly on her back towards the rear will usually have the same effect. Even if you have only another bitch you will probably be able to tell by her antics whether she is ready or not, as she will ride another bitch if there is one about.

The selection of the right day for mating a bitch is very important. This is when the bitch has ovulated and there are the greatest number of eggs available in the Fallopian tubes ready for fertilisation by the sperm of the dog. Too early or too late results in a small litter, though in some cases where a bitch habitually has small litters a hormone injection can be of great benefit.

Apart from the obvious signs of when a bitch is ready for mating, it is possible to diagnose this by means of Tes-tape such as is used by diabetics. A small piece is inserted into the vagina, and if it turns green this indicates that the bitch is ready. This is because glucose is secreted in the vagina at the time of ovulation.

If you are in any doubt and may have missed the onset of the season, your vet can take a swab from the vagina and if he has a microscope he will be able to tell you immediately whether your bitch is ready for mating or not. This is invaluable if you intend to take a long journey to a dog.

If during previous seasons you have been in the habit of using an 'anti-mate' preparation on your bitch, do not do so during the season in which you intend to breed from her. I have had people arrive with bitches strongly smelling of 'Keep Away' or something similar and even my nostrils have been able to detect it, let alone the dog's. I am not suggesting that it would be enough to deter most stud dogs, but it would do nothing to help a shy or inexperienced young dog.

One word of warning on your arrival at the home of the stud dog you are visiting. Do not drive up to the front door and jump out of the car followed by dogs and children. It very often happens that there are old age pensioners – doggy ones – somewhere in the vicinity, or even a stud dog at large. This happened to me once when a car suddenly arrived and out shot mother, father, children and several dogs, including a black Labrador who rushed up to my own dog with hackles raised, intent on showing who was boss. Mercifully my dog was very tolerant and I was able to call him away and pop him into my car nearby before the situation got out of hand, but this thoughtless action could have provoked a very nasty fight. Never take your dogs out of your car when visiting other kennels unless you are invited to do so. There is also the possibility of bringing infection and some breeders are particularly nervous of running any risk. Even though all their dogs are probably inoculated there are other diseases which can be carried through the urine and it is easy to see how quickly infection can be spread.

Although it is quite common for bitches of the smaller breeds to be sent in travelling boxes by train to the stud dog, I do not think that many Goldens are sent by train today. There was a time, however, when I often received bitches in season sent just on a chain in the guard's van, and after service I sent them back in the same way. Provided that it was a through train and they were met at the other end there seemed no risk involved. However, I should not feel very happy about using this method today.

Before the bitch is introduced to the dog it is as well for her to have the opportunity of relieving herself. Then she can be put straight back in the kennel after service and be kept quiet, or put into her owner's car.

The stud fee should have been agreed upon when the appointment was made, and this should be paid before taking the bitch away. This fee is paid for the service of the dog, and not as an insurance that the bitch will have puppies. It is therefore not obligatory that a free service is given if she does not produce a litter, but most breeders do so. If there are no puppies it is not necessarily the dog's fault, as there are many reasons why this can happen. The bitch may have been brought to the dog too early or too late. She may be too fat, which is the most frequent cause of missing, or she may be out of condition or emaciate ˙

It is sometimes agreed that the owner of the stud dog shall take the pick of a litter instead of a fee, but this is generally to oblige the owner of the bitch and is by no means a regular occurrence, so it should not be expected as a matter of course.

After the mating the dog's pedigree should be handed over before the bitch leaves the premises. If the dog is used regularly at stud the pedigree is usually printed on a 'stud card', together with the dog's date of birth and registration number.

The owner of the bitch should be careful not to let her out without supervision for at least another week. The fact that she has been mated will not prevent her from mating again if she has the opportunity, and her litter may then include two sets of puppies, differing considerably in appearance, and perhaps not even born on the same day. Even if the puppies are apparently Goldens, such a litter cannot be registered as pure bred, and a stud fee has been wasted.

It is, however, an old wives' tale that a misalliance with a dog of a different breed will spoil a bitch for future breeding of pure bred litters. I once bought an adult bitch and after I had had her for about six weeks I began to suspect that she was in whelp. This had no sooner occurred to me than I went out the next morning to find that she had produced ten black puppies during the night. Everything was spotlessly clean and all the puppies were alive and sucking lustily.

I have never been so taken aback as I was on this occasion. Even though I had begun to suspect that she was in whelp she had shown no signs of being so advanced, and had the evening before been galloping over the fields quite happily. On inquiry from the previous owner I found that she had been sent to a Keeper's kennels whilst in season. Evidently he had a black Labrador dog.

When I mated her the next time she produced an excellent litter with the same ease. All Goldens this time, but by a strange coincidence one puppy had a very small black fleck in it.

The Service

It is commonly thought by those who have had no experience of dog breeding that to mate a bitch is a simple matter and requires only that the dog be introduced to the bitch and if left together all will be well. Although a large number of matings takes place very easily there are many bitches who would never be mated at all if some help were not given. It requires a lot of patience, time and 'know how' to bring about a satisfactory service if the bitch is nervous or unwilling. Often a bitch's temperament at this time is quite different from that of her normal behaviour. She may be upset by the strange surroundings and will defend herself against any advances by the dog.

Generally the most difficult bitches to mate are pet bitches who have not been accustomed to mixing with other dogs, and their owners are quite shocked at their behaviour.

The dog and the bitch should be given time to get used to each other, as a natural mating is always preferable. But if it becomes obvious that no progress is being made then action should be taken to control the bitch, so that the whole operation is completed as quickly as possible, rather than allow the bitch to continue to be distressed and the dog frustrated.

Do not use a young and inexperienced dog on a bitch of this type or he may be permanently put off.

The owner of the bitch can do much to assist if he will hold the bitch's head and talk soothingly to her whilst the dog mounts her.

If she continues to turn on the dog then as a last resort take a bandage and place over the muzzle and cross under the chin. Bring the ends up and tie behind the ears. The owner should now hold the head firmly and if necessary between his knees. The dog will now have confidence knowing that she cannot turn on him. The stud dog's owner will probably have to hold the bitch up to prevent her sitting on her hind-quarters.

If the dog is experienced and trained to expect some assistance he will be successful in a very few minutes, which is far better than prolonging the courtship over several days with both dog and bitch upset and in all probability no success in the end. Mating a bitch is often a game of patience. If you are not successful after trying for some time and there is a danger of the dog wearing himself out, it is always a good idea to separate the pair and let them have a rest out of sight of each other. Often the dog will come back with renewed vigour and mate her right away. The behaviour of each stud dog varies considerably and they cannot all be treated alike. If possible get him used from the start to your holding the bitch and if he does not resent this you will be able to assist him a lot by helping him to negotiate and penetrate the vulva of the bitch by placing your hand underneath the bitch and holding it towards the penis of the dog. Once contact has been made the dog will usually penetrate straight away.

If the dog jumps down immediately you stoop down to help him, it is a game of patience, as he may fumble about for a long while before making contact. In this case it sometimes helps to cut a little of the feathering off around the vulva in order to make contact easier, and to smear the vulva with vaseline.

In some cases the young dog is shy and does not appreciate an audience. In order to encourage him if it is his first bitch go out of the room but keep an eye on him if possible through a window.

I am frequently told of bitches who have never been able to be bred from, and on enquiry I have found that the owners have tried to use a dog who has never mated a bitch before or has had little experience, and that in most cases they have left them to their own devices and hoped for the best.

On no account should the two be left alone and unobserved. In the first place you could never be sure if a mating has taken place or not, which is an unsatisfactory state of affairs anyway. Also you would not be able to charge a stud fee unless you had witnessed a tie between the two. But possibly more important still is the fact that they can quite easily injure each other by trying to pull apart.

Once the dog has completed the service he will relax and slide down off the bitch's back and if the dog does not do it himself he should be 'turned'. This in fact is a matter of lifting the dog's hind leg over the back of the bitch so that they stand tail to tail.

Some dogs do this themselves as it is the most comfortable position for them to be in. Be sure that a tie has actually taken place or the dog may slip out and although a tie is not essential it is necessary if a fee is being charged. It is quite possible for the bitch to conceive if the dog is held in position but it is not desirable.

Once the bitch discovers that she cannot get away from the dog she may panic and struggle. It is essential that someone, preferably the owner, should be at hand to calm her down. On no account should she be allowed to sit down. Not only can she rupture the dog but she will cause herself a lot of unnecessary discomfort. It is usual for the tie to take from ten to twenty minutes but this varies considerably and I have known it to take two hours but this is exceptional.

As soon as the two come apart the bitch should be put back in the kennel to rest for a while or put in the owner's car whilst the final business is attended to.

A second mating may be desirable if the first did not appear wholly successful, such as a very short tie or no tie at all. Once the dog has penetrated the bitch, the same dog must be used and no other dog as it is possible that some semen actually passed from the dog to the bitch even if the contact was very brief. If two dogs mate the same bitch accidentally the resulting puppies must have the names of both sires placed on the pedigree and reported to the Kennel Club before they can be registered.

After a good mating a second service is by no means essential but some owners of bitches will ask for it. If so this should not take place for forty-eight hours as any semen from the first service will remain active for this time. No extra charge is made, and should there be no resulting litter a free service is generally offered the next time the bitch comes in season. The fee charged is for the service and is payable at the time and not (as some people think) when the puppies arrive, unless the owner of the dog has some doubt about his fertility or is proving an untried dog.

Care of the Brood Bitch

Bitches are usually in full coat when they come into season and generally look their best. They should be kept in good hard condition and not allowed to get fat. It is very easy for bitches to put on weight and it is not so easy to get them back into condition. At all times their diet should be regulated to suit them.

The period of gestation is sixty-three days, although a maiden bitch usually whelps two or three days early but if the puppies arrive as much as a week early their chance of survival is not great. Similarly they can and often do arrive two or three days late when it is an older bitch.

Not until the bitch has been in whelp for five or six weeks can you be positive that she is in whelp. They can be very deceiving but the person who knows the bitch well can usually tell by her behaviour. Sometimes a bitch will go off her food for a few days at three weeks and even show signs of sickness. This soon passes and the appetite generally increases.

Her normal diet should be kept to until you are sure that she is in whelp at about six weeks when she should be given a morning and evening feed and for the last two weeks a pint of milk at midday with a raw egg added.

From the day that she was mated she should have additional calcium added to her food. There are various forms of this on the market.

She should be exercised regularly every day as usual but not encouraged to jump, and towards the end not permitted to play roughly with other dogs.

At no time should she be tired out and towards the last week she will pant quite a lot and lie down outstretched on her side. It is possible to see the movement of the puppies in this position.

As the last few days approach it is a good idea to give her a teaspoonful of liquid paraffin. This helps to keep her regular without undue straining.

Some people like to worm their bitches whilst they are in whelp but this should not be done after the third week. I am not a great advocate of this myself. If the bitch has been well looked after prior to mating and kept free of worms I do not think there is much to be gained. For the last few nights she should be put to sleep in the room or kennel in which the whelping box has been placed ready for the great event.

A day or so before the puppies are due to arrive the bitch should be prepared for whelping by being thoroughly groomed so that she is as clean as possible. The long hair at her rear should be trimmed back a little so that there is no danger of a puppy being caught up in it and strangled, which in long-haired breeds is quite easily done.

Whelping and Care of Young Puppies

As a general rule Golden Retrievers whelp quite easily and do not need much assistance. However, there are times when everything is not normal and it is as well to be able to recognise this situation.

It is important that the bitch should be provided with a good-sized whelping box. So often people are apt to make do with the bed she is used to, forgetting that she will need extra room for herself and her family – and it is surprising just how quickly the puppies grow. Also the bitch needs room to manoeuvre whilst she is having the puppies, otherwise there is a risk of some of them being lain on. I suggest a box four foot by three foot, with the sides nine inches deep. The box should not be raised off the floor, and I like the front board to be moveable, so that when the puppies are three weeks old this can be removed and they can go outside the box to be clean. A whelping rail can also be fitted if desired.

The use of an infra red ray lamp at all times of the year is invaluable. In the height of summer it may not be necessary to keep it on for more than a few hours, but certainly whilst the bitch is whelping and until all the puppies are dry. We seldom have it so hot that the comfort a lamp gives is not appreciated by the bitch. At most times of the year it can be kept on day and night when the puppies are very young. They will be much more content and consequently grow more quickly. The lamp should be hung about three feet six inches above the bed. A dull emitter is very much better than a bright one as it is more restful for the bitch and less trying for the eyes of the puppies than a bright light.

Do not put blankets on the bed as the bitch will naturally want to scratch up her bed before she actually has the puppies. Not only will the blankets be torn, but they constitute a danger to the puppies when they do arrive, as they can easily be suffocated by getting underneath them, or be caught up and possibly strangled in the loose threads. Most people use newspaper in the bed for the bitch to whelp on, but I prefer to use hessian nailed down at the corners with flat headed drugget pins. This gives the puppies more purchase to push themselves towards the mother, and she cannot scratch it up.

This has become increasingly difficult to obtain, but fortunately a new synthetic material, which is marketed under various different names such as 'Vetbed', 'Snugrug' or 'Petbed', has come on the market and is excellent. It has a fluffy appearance but allows all moisture to go through it to be absorbed by newspaper underneath. It is very hygienic and can be easily machine washed. The warmth of this material has a comforting effect on both bitch and puppies. However I would not put this in the whelping bed for the first two or three days if the bitch has a heavy discharge.

When the bitch is about to whelp she usually goes off her food, and if she does take a little milk she will probably be sick. It will be noticed that she is shivering and her temperature will often drop from the normal 101.5 to below 100 degrees.

Most bitches are best left quiet and undisturbed at this stage, with frequent visits just to see that all is well and provide reassurance if she seems to need it. Once she can be seen to be straining it is reasonable to expect the first puppy to be born within the next hour. If the bitch continues to strain and no puppy is born then it is time to investigate and some help may be necessary. The puppy should protrude from the vulva head first with its front legs under its chin. If after continued straining no progress is made then take a piece of towelling, grip the puppy gently but firmly, and as the bitch strains draw it carefully forward. It will then probably slip out quite easily.

It will be noticed that the puppy is enveloped in a membrane and is attached by the umbilical cord to the placenta or 'after-birth', which should be delivered immediately after the puppy. If it is the bitch's first litter she may not know what to do next, and if no one is there may ignore the puppy entirely. Move it up to her head and she will in all probability start to lick away the membrane. This she does by instinct and soon the puppy will breathe air for the first time. The bitch will then chew the umbilical cord and free the puppy from the placenta which she will consume. This is quite a natural thing for her to do but it so disgusts some people that they prevent the bitch from doing so. It also causes a black diarrhoea for a day or so. Personally I prefer my bitches to do what comes naturally, and after they have cleaned up the first puppy and it has begun to suck they quickly learn what they have to do with the subsequent ones.

It sometimes happens that two or three puppies are born quite easily and then nothing happens and the bitch stops straining. This is what is called uterine inertia and the vet must be asked to call as soon as possible. He will probably give her an injection of pituitary extract which will start the contractions again. If this does not have the desired effect and no more puppies arrive it will probably mean a Caesarian operation. Uterine inertia arises most often in older bitches who get tired and give up in the middle of whelping. This is the reason why I am so against bitches over seven years of age being bred from, or even younger ones if this condition has been experienced in a previous litter, as it is a warning.

Sometimes the puppy's hind legs appear first. This is known as breech presentation, and when it occurs some help may be necessary, particularly if the water bag has broken. It is essential that the whelp is born without delay, otherwise it is likely to be drowned or asphyxiated. As the legs are too slippery to hold, a piece of towelling or cotton wool should be used to grasp them firmly, and they should then be drawn steadily forwards and downwards. If there are no contractions and there is difficulty in getting the puppy away a little liquid paraffin syringed into the vagina will help to lubricate it.

It is not often that Golden Retrievers have problems at whelping time, as do breeds with large heads such as the bull breeds, but it is as well to be prepared for the unexpected, particularly with a first litter or a bitch who is new to you.

I offer the bitch a drink of warm milk whilst she is whelping, as it is an exhausting process and a little refreshment between the arrival of each puppy is seldom refused.

If all is seen to be going well it is not necessary to stay with her all the time, but frequent visits must be made as it may be necessary to revive a puppy which the bitch has neglected to attend to. This is done by massaging the body and breathing slowly into its mouth. It is really quite amazing to see the little body come to life. Wrapped up in a warm towel and massaged the puppy may soon be sucking and taking a firm hold of life.

If by any chance a puppy has got away from its mother or has been pushed aside and is cold, a good way of reviving it is to place it in a warm oven. This sounds drastic but it has saved many a puppy's life and there are many dogs winning today who owe their lives to being warmed up in the oven. Even more drastic but very effective is to plunge the puppy into a basin of hot water, holding his head above the surface. The water should be several degrees above blood heat. If the puppy is held in it for about a minute, then rubbed with a towel and placed in the oven the results are quite miraculous.

Do not give up even if a puppy looks dead when born. It may be that the water bag broke before the puppy was delivered, thus causing it to be almost drowned, so try holding the puppy up by its hind-quarters with its head hanging down, and with the other hand move the front legs backwards and forwards. If there is any mucus coming from its mouth clear this away with a piece of cotton wool, open its mouth and draw the tongue down. Sometimes this is stuck to the roof of the mouth. Now breathe gently down the throat. You will get the biggest thrill you ever had if the puppy suddenly gives a little gasp and you know that your efforts have not been in vain. A few more life-giving breaths and your puppy will be taking hold of life and getting stronger every second.

Finally when the bitch has produced perhaps eight or ten puppies and all are sucking contentedly she will look more relaxed and will probably sleep. It is obvious then that she has completed her task, as if any puppies are left it is usual for her to be restless. In this case, or if in any doubt, get your vet to give her an examination not later than the next day to make sure that none have been left behind, as this can cause a very dangerous and often fatal condition.

When the bitch has had a good rest I encourage her to go out and relieve herself. Whilst she is out of the room a clean piece of paper or hessian can be placed in the box and the puppies can be examined to identify their sex.

Keep her on a very light diet for the next two days and give her plenty of fluid. I make a point of visiting the bitch every three hours during the first two nights after the puppies have been born. I regard these as the most crucial, and if any puppies begin to fade it is usually during the second night. If there is a weak one you will be able to detect this by the plaintive cry it gives, and although it may hang on to life for two days it usually succumbs on the second night despite all your efforts to try and save it.

During the night the bitch will get up and change her position so that the puppies suck from the other side and the milk is drawn off evenly from all her teats. On the third day the milk will be flowing freely if she has had plenty of liquid to drink. Very often the temperature rises a little on this day, and a watch should be kept to see that all the teats are soft and that there is no sign of mastitis.

It is quite usual for the bitch to have some discharge from the vagina for two or three weeks after whelping. But should this remain very dark in colour after the first two or three days it is best to call the vet who will probably give her an antibiotic injection to clear up the possible infection. If the bitch has had a bad time whelping and the puppies have been delayed or some have been born dead a thick black discharge often follows. This is very unpleasant and if allowed to remain will cause severe soreness on the bitch's hind-quarters and the hair will come off.

The day after whelping when the bitch is feeling more herself I always wash down her hind-quarters with soap and disinfectant, making sure to rub her down thoroughly so that she is as dry as possible before she goes back to the puppies. Once underneath the lamp she will soon dry.

If all is well on the third day the bitch will now be able to have raw meat and soaked biscuit meal as well as milk foods and cereal. I recommend the following diet:

8 a.m. 1 pint of milk with glucose or honey and a little Farex added.

10 a.m. 1 pound of meat and as much soaked biscuit meal as she will readily eat. Gradually increase the quantity as the puppies get older and make more demands on her.

2 p.m. 1 pint of milk which can be made up as an egg custard or milk pudding.

6 p.m. Repeat the 10 a.m. feed.

11.30 p.m. 1 pint of milk with glucose or honey added and an egg.

The milk produced by the bitch for the first few days is called Colostrum and contains antibodies which will protect the puppies from any infection. Throughout the bitch's lactation whilst the puppies are still feeding from her they are reasonably safe, though inoculation will be needed later to protect them. (See 'Distemper')

At three to four days old, when the puppies havs really taken a hold of life and are sucking lustily and growing daily, they should be inspected individually to make sure that the umbilical cord has dried up and fallen off. Occasionally the wound does not heal well, particularly if the bitch has bitten the cord off too close to the body of the puppy. In this case it may become infected and eventually cause the puppy to die. If the wound has not healed it should be treated with an antiseptic such as Gentian Violet or some form of penicillin.

Whilst handling the puppies make sure that none are malformed. This is rare but occasionally a puppy may have a twisted tail, a deformed leg, or a toe missing. If it is likely to cause much disfigurement or discomfort it is better to dispose of the puppy at once. This should be done professionally.

Now is the time to remove the dew-claws if you are going to do it at all. I do not remove them and I know of few Golden Retriever breeders who do, but it is entirely optional. If they are not removed a careful check should be made from time to time to see that the claws do not grow too long as they can become a nuisance by catching in things. Sometimes they break off or can be badly torn. Neglected dew-claws can also grow round and into the leg, though it is hard to believe that anyone would allow this to happen.

For the first week after whelping the bitch will not want to leave the puppies much and will have to be encouraged even to go out and relieve herself. She should be kept as quiet as possible and in no circumstances should any other dogs be able to invade her privacy.

Never take the bitch right away from her puppies at any time. If possible leave the door of her kennel open so that she can go in and out if she wants to, but let her decide this. A bitch can become very upset and worried if parted from her young, and nothing could be worse for the flow of milk which could dry up altogether if she is very disturbed.

I was quite horrified when I received a phone call from someone whose bitch had recently whelped and she asked me if it was really necessary for her to be taken for a walk each day as her vet had recommended. Apparently she was having the greatest difficulty in getting the bitch away from the puppies and she was very unwilling to go for a walk. I can only think that the vet was very young and inexperienced. Perhaps he thought that what was right for a cow or horse must necessarily be right for a dog.

Having produced a large family a bitch's first instinct is to keep them warm and clean and enable them to suckle from her. This they need to do at frequent short intervals and on no account should they be separated from their mother. She also needs to lie quietly to regain her own strength, as she will probably be very exhaused for a few days.

I once saw a bitch who had a very large litter of two weeks old being taken shopping in the town. What stupidity. A bitch may be happy to leave her babies for five or ten minutes at this age, but to take her for a walk is quite unnecessary and unkind.

Puppies need to suck about every two hours at least, and if the litter is a large one it sometimes means that they have to take it in turns at the milk bar. The bitch will know instinctively and by the fullness of her teats when the puppies need feeding, but if there are any small or weak ones a watch should be kept to see that they get their fair share.

By the time the puppies are three weeks old they can be taught to lap, and this should be done to lessen the demands which they are now making on their mother. Having decided on the type of milk food you are going to rear them on, mix some with a little glucose or honey added and put it into a very shallow dish on some newspaper on the floor. The paper is to prevent them getting sawdust into the milk, as they will put their feet into the dish if not watched, at any rate while they are learning the ropes. Place the puppies round the dish and if necessary push their noses into it to start them lapping. Do this once a day for the first three days and then increase it to twice a day by the time they are four weeks old.

At four weeks thicken the milk slightly with Farex or similar baby cereal and feed three times a day, giving them as much as they will readily clear up. Towards the end of the fourth week replace one milk feed by one of soaked fine biscuit meal and raw minced beef.

Assuming that there are eight or ten puppies in the litter I would put down two or possibly three dishes spreading the puppies equally round them. I am a great believer in communal feeding. It is the natural method and I believe that competition is good and makes each puppy eat up well. I have never owned a fussy feeder. I always stand by and see that none are pushed out and that all get a fair share.

I make a point of visiting as many litters by my stud dogs as possible, and the biggest mistake I find people make is not that the owners do not give their puppies the best food but that they do not give them enough.

Almost every breeder has his or her own set diet for rearing puppies. I stick to the simple principle of meat and biscuit night and morning, with egg and milk at midday and last thing at night. By the time the puppies are six weeks old they should be having a morning and evening feed of meat and biscuit soaked in gravy, Oxo, Bovril or Marmite, and at midday and last thing at night they should have at least six fluid ounces of milk each, to which Farex and raw egg have been added. This amount should be increased accordingly as they grow older.

For the moment the bitch will still be supplying a little and I always keep my bitches with their litter at night until the puppies are six weeks old. A bench should be provided in the kennel on to which a bitch can jump out of the way of the puppies as she will not want to have them pulling at her all the time, and it is very unkind to leave her with no means of escape from them.

On the other hand I hear people say time and again that their bitch did not want to stay with the puppies at night after they were about four weeks old, and that they have allowed her to come back indoors to sleep, or have put her in a separate kennel. I think that this is a dreadful mistake. What the bitch really wanted was to be able to get away from the puppies when they pestered her, but during the night and early morning she would have jumped down from her bench and fed them. For her own comfort she needs to feed them. At this age the milk flow is at its height and the puppies are drawing off a considerable amount even though they may be having supplementary milk feeds.

Another reason why a bitch may show signs of not wanting to stay with her puppies is that their claws have become sharp and require cutting. This can be done very successfully with a pair of nail clippers. Great care should be taken to avoid cutting off too much as this will cause some pain and bleeding.

Some people like to worm their puppies at about a month old. This depends entirely on what type of worm medicine is used and is a matter of opinion. It also depends on the condition of the puppies. If they look distended then the sooner they are done the better, especially if they have a variable appetite and do not seem to be thriving as they should. I do not usually worm mine before they are six weeks old, and then again ten days

A healthy young puppy at play.

later. It is very important to be thorough and weigh each puppy and dose him according to weight. I like to worm puppies twice before they leave the kennel, and recommend that they are wormed again when they are twelve weeks old.

If the bitch is allowed to visit the puppies whenever she wishes she will automatically wean them and her teats will go back to normal shape. At six weeks, when she no longer sleeps with them, I put her in with them for about five minutes before I give the puppies their last feed, and again in the morning I let her in with them for a few minutes before feeding them. She will probably visit them again at midday for a few days, then gradually reduce it to a visit in the morning only, until it is obvious that there is no need for her to go to them at all.

Once the puppies are having four meals a day the bitch's own diet can be reduced, but not before. Gradually reduce the size of the meals and cut out the early morning milk and the milk given last thing at night. If she has been well looked after she should not look poor or run down. When the puppies are about twelve weeks old she will probably go into a moult and will lose all her feathering as well as body coat. But by the time the puppies are about five or six months old she will have grown a lovely new coat and will come in season again.

Line Breeding

I have been asked to add a note on line breeding. This is the practice of mating a bitch to a dog with whom she has an outstanding grandparent or great-grandparent in common, so that there is a dominant influence in the strain, as opposed to a complete outcross where there are no common factors. It should not be confused with in-breeding, where both parents have similar or identical heredity and no fresh strain is introduced.

Given a sound strain, line breeding is extremely successful, but full knowledge of all the qualities of preceding generations is needed, as any faults in these would also be accentuated.

7 Accidents, Ailments and Remedies

Accidents

Under this heading there are various types of accident, the most common being those in the home and those on the road which take such a toll.

Puppies which are reared in the home are much more likely to be involved in accidents than those reared in a kennel where there are not likely to be so many hazards. In a home it is inevitable that a puppy will explore pulling things off shelves and tables. None of them are little angels and their natural inquisitiveness may lead them into danger.

There is nothing a Golden likes better than to lie with his back up against the kitchen stove, if it is the type which is warm day and night. Cooking with dogs in close proximity does present the danger of scalding with boiling water, food or fat, so extra care should be taken to avoid such a tragedy.

Should such an event occur, pour cold water over the dog immediately to lessen the heat. If you have ice cubes available add these to the water and continue swabbing until medical help arrives. When fat or hot frying oil has been spilt over the dog it is necessary to take quick action before this penetrates to the skin, so try to scrape it off with the back of a knife in the same direction as the hair grows. Having done so, swab with cold water. Make an emergency call to your vet and keep the dog as quiet as possible until he comes. Be sure to tell him the nature of the accident so that he comes prepared.

Gas taps, electric plugs and cables are also potential dangers, and many a puppy has lost his life through chewing the flex of an electric appliance. Needless to say one should never leave a dog in a room alone with plugged-in appliances or an unguarded fire.

Road accidents often mean broken bones and the dog will have to be taken to your vet's surgery. If there is severe haemorrhage first aid treatment should be carried out by applying pressure to the wound and bandaging a pad over it. If this does not alleviate it a tourniquet must be applied. In most cases it is a leg which is involved and if the bleeding is severe this probably means that an artery or vein has been severed. In such a case a nylon stocking or handkerchief is as good as anything to wind round the leg above the wound. Find some object such as the handle of a spoon or a pencil to put through the loop of the bandage in order to twist it and tighten the pressure to stop the flow of blood. This can be a life saver, as the dog who loses a great deal of blood will be severely shocked and shock can be fatal.

The tourniquet should be loosened every fifteen minutes to prevent damage to the blood vessels or gangrene may be caused. It should not be applied unless it is obvious that the animal is losing a lot of blood and drastic action must be taken. This should only be attempted by a responsible person.

Care should be taken in moving a dog who has been involved in an accident. Help should be sought as one person alone cannot do this without the risk of causing further injury. It is best to lay the dog on a board if one is available, but if not, a rug or even a sack will do. Lift the corners and carry it to the car, preferably an estate car so that the dog can lie flat.

If a leg is obviously broken it should be immobilised by applying a splint before the dog is moved. A stick tied to the leg at the top and bottom will prevent movement and cause less pain.

Accidents in the field are frequent in summer time when agricultural machinery is in action either cutting grass or harvesting. I have been rung up more than once by people urgently wanting to replace dogs who have had their legs amputated by mowing machines, usually because the dog has been allowed to follow when cutting is in progress and chase rabbits as they bolt. The lives of untrained dogs are put in peril when they are allowed to do this.

I once knew a Golden with three legs which was the result of a shooting accident. It does sometimes happen, too, that a dog gets staked when jumping a hedge, or caught up in wire. I have seen both things happen in the shooting field. One of my own dogs received a six-inch three-cornered tear on its flank through being caught on the protruding screw of a straining wire. One would hardly think that such a thing could happen, but the dog's coat was literally skinned off it and required over thirty stitches to draw it together. Pig wire can cause trouble unless jumped cleanly. I saw a Golden hung up by his hind leg when jumping a fence of this kind. One hind leg slipped so that the second row of wire became twisted over the top row which meant that the dog's hind leg was trapped. In this position he was helpless and resented interference. The only way to release him was by lifting him back over the fence; the dog, with normally the sweetest nature, was so frightened that he bit his owner's arm in the process.

Many accidents can be avoided by proper training of the dog and watchfulness on the part of his owner. If an accident does occur, a calm and unflurried handling of the situation, whatever one's private feelings, can help to give the dog confidence and the maximum chance of recovery.

Common Ailments and Diseases

ANAL GLANDS

These are two small glands situated at the entrance to the anus. They sometimes cause distress to the dog who will rub his rear parts along the ground to relieve the irritation. Veterinary advice should be sought as the glands will require squeezing out. Some dogs seem to need regular attention in this respect otherwise abscesses will result.

ANAL PROLAPSIS

This sometimes happens in puppies and is generally due to undue straining or being badly infected with worms. The protruding part should be replaced as quickly as possible, and if the condition recurs professional advice should be sought.

CANKER

This is caused by a mite and is accompanied by a dark brown discharge causing intense irritation. The dog usually holds his head on one side or puts his paw up to the affected ear. There are many good remedies on the market which if used regularly will ensure that the ears are quite clean. Canker in ears which have been neglected can become chronic and in some cases impossible to cure.

COCCIDIOSIS

This is a highly infectious disease in which the dog will lose condition. He will suffer from diarrhoea in which there will be traces of blood. This disease usually attacks poultry and as the spores are in the droppings it is not wise to keep dogs where poultry have been or allow them to pick up poultry droppings.

CYSTS

These can appear on the body or as interdigital cysts between the toes. Golden Retrievers do not seem as prone to them as most breeds. They take the form of a boil and their presence generally denotes that a dog is out of condition and needs some form of tonic. Often a complete change of diet will help.

   This is a most painful condition and if the cyst is between the toes the dog will go lame and is seen constantly licking his foot. This should be bathed in an antiseptic solution. After a few days the cyst will burst and the inflammation gradually subside.

DIABETES

Usually distinguished by an abnormal thirst. Although the animal continues to eat well he will lose condition and become excessively thin. If the urine is tested it will reveal an excessive amount of sugar. The disease sometimes attacks middle-aged dogs, but more frequently older dogs when the chance of a cure is slight. However, as with human beings, diet can be adjusted and insulin injections can be given.

DIARRHOEA

If this is accompanied by a rise in temperature a veterinary surgeon should be consulted. It may, however, be caused by worms, particularly in puppies, or by eating something which has upset the digestion. Usually the dog will go off his food, and in this case the dog knows best. Generally there is no cause for alarm and by the following day he will show interest in food again, but only milk food should be offered, mixed with a little kaolin, or arrowroot made up into a creamy thickness. This diet should be continued until the motions become formed again.

DISTEMPER, HARD PAD, HEPATITIS, AND LEPTOSPIROSIS

These serious diseases are the scourge of the dog world. They are, however, far less menacing than they used to be owing to modern vaccines. Fortunately the pet owner is more conscious of these nowadays and takes advantage of the inoculations available.

The diseases can be picked up in many ways and the most scrupulously careful breeder may be faced with an outbreak through no fault in general management or negligence. Foxes, rats, fleas, lice and birds can bring the virus to the kennel, but if the inmates have all been inoculated the attack is only likely to be mild and in some cases hardly noticeable, the adults going off colour in turn for perhaps only twenty-four hours. The attack may be accompanied by sickness and diarrhoea when of course correct diagnosis must be sought and proper precautions taken. Even a mild attack can leave its mark on those affected. (See 'Hepatitis')

Although not everyone is in agreement with inoculations, some preferring natural rearing methods and herbs, vaccines have reached such a high stage of perfection that they seldom have a breakdown. If inoculation is properly carried out with booster injections when necessary the dog should have a lifetime of protection.

At the onset of distemper the dog will lose his appetite and have diarrhoea and vomiting. The temperature will rise to 103 or 104 degrees. The eyes will be blurred with a yellow discharge seeping from the corners, and the disease is generally distinguished by a harsh cough. In any case of suspected distemper the dog should be isolated from any others, and veterinary advice should be sought at once. The dog should meanwhile be kept warm and as quiet as possible, as any exercising at this stage can result in complications later.

Young puppies still sucking from their dam receive natural protection through a substance called Colostrum which is absorbed from the bitch's milk. Until the puppy is fully weaned it is fairly well protected. There is an injection which some people take advantage of which can be given at eight weeks old, but this is only effective for a month, when immunisation should be carried out.

It is a matter of choice which vaccine is used for immunisation as there are several makes on the market and it is up to the owner to decide which diseases he wishes his dog to be immunised against. Burroughs Wellcome & Co. have several vaccines available. Their Epivax T.C. is for use against distemper and hard-pad, whilst Epivax T.C. Plus includes contagious hepatitis as well. Epivax Double Plus includes the above mentioned diseases as well as *Leptospira canicola* and *Leptospira icterohaemorrhagiae*(Jaundice). Some people whose dogs are never likely to come into contact with rats or run where rats have urinated do not deem the Double Plus injection necessary. For continuous immunity against Leptospirosis a booster injection of Leptovax Plus is necessary from time to time.

At all costs care should be taken to avoid these diseases. Even if the patient is cured, which will in any case have caused a lot of worry and additional expense, the animal is seldom quite the same afterwards. Nervous disorders may be left, like Chorea which is a rhythmic twitching very distressing to watch and impossible to cure. Other weaknesses are also apparent, sometimes in the hind-quarters, and generally the teeth are left badly discoloured. Sometimes the dog becomes blind.

HARD PAD
This is a similar virus to distemper, the main difference being that the feet swell and the pads harden and crack.

HEPATITIS
This is sometimes known as Rubarth's disease. It is a highly infectious killer disease and those dogs which are lucky enough to survive are generally left with some after effects, one of which is that often bitches will in future produce 'fading puppies' and in turn any surviving puppies from that litter will also produce fading puppies in a vicious circle. In such circumstances it is not economical to try to breed from bitches so affected as it leads only to great disappointment.

LEPTOSPIROSIS
There are two forms of this disease, leptospiral jaundice and leptospiral

canicola. Although it is not easy to distinguish the difference the one attacks the liver causing jaundice, and the virus called canicola attacks the kidneys. Inoculation covers both types. As rats are largely responsible for the spread of these diseases strict hygiene should be observed and rats should be eliminated as far as possible. No food should ever be left down in a kennel to attract them and all stores should be kept in covered metal bins to avoid contamination. I do not feel that one can be too careful on this point as leptospirosis can also be contracted by human beings through contact with infected urine from rats, and it is possible to touch something which has been contaminated without being aware of it. It is a serious disease and sometimes fatal.

ECLAMPSIA

This condition is brought about by a sudden deficiency of calcium and is sometimes experienced by nursing bitches of particularly large litters which can be a drain on natural secretion. The bitch pants a great deal and staggers about with a dazed expression and often falls down and is unable to rise. A vet must be called at once who will inject heavy doses of calcium. She should be moved away from her puppies until she has recovered sufficiently. She will require further doses of calcium and liberal amounts of calcium mixed with her food. This state of affairs can usually be avoided if care has been taken to give some form of calcium during pregnancy and lactation.

As a result of eclampsia it is wise to wean the puppies or at least supplement their feeding as much as possible to relieve the strain on the bitch. An attack may develop about the third day after whelping or more usually when the puppies are about three or four weeks old when the greatest strain is experienced by the bitch trying to provide milk for a large family. In this instance I would advise getting the puppies to lap as soon as possible or bottle feeding some of them, particularly any smaller puppies.

ECZEMA

There are several kinds of eczema which are generally conditional and not infectious.

Wet Eczema starts with an eruption which exudes moisture. In Golden Retrievers this generally appears under the ear flaps or around the neck, although it can appear anywhere on the body. A complete change of diet is recommended and all carbohydrates cut down or left out of the diet completely for a while. It usually occurs during the hottest weather in the latter part of the year and is a malady which most Goldens have once in a lifetime even if only slightly. I have found some bitches have a patch of eczema about a month before coming into season as regularly as clockwork whilst others may have one bad attack and never have another. Wet eczema spreads so quickly it can be quite alarming to one who has never seen it and in this case veterinary advice must be sought as the glands can become affected and the dog really ill. If the first sign of a wet patch is treated there is nothing to worry about. (See 'Remedies: peroxide of hydrogen')

Dry Eczema. This starts with a red patch which the dog scratches continually and is often caused by worms or over feeding or alternatively by being in poor health generally and under nourishment. The dog should be treated internally to get to the root of the trouble. This disease is often confused with mange which differs greatly being highly infectious. (See 'Mange')

EPILEPSY

This is a condition in which the dog froths at the mouth and clamps his jaws. The whole body stiffens and the limbs are extended. After a few minutes the dog will relax and start moving his legs as if trying to run, at the same time he will probably lose control of his bladder and bowels. The duration of a fit varies but in most cases the dog will quieten down within ten minutes and lie in a dazed state. When he tries to get up he will be very unsteady on his feet.

There is very little one can do in these cases except to keep the dog as quiet as possible in a darkened room and call the vet, who will administer a sedative. A dog who is subject to having fits gives little warning of the onset but they usually follow a pattern of regular intervals.

FADING PUPPIES

Nothing can compare with the disappointment experienced when a whole litter of apparently healthy puppies fades out after two or three days. These may have been whelped quite easily and everything normal. Gradually one or two will stop sucking and set up a cry which is called 'gulling'. This is so called because it sounds like the noise which gulls make when they are hungry. The puppies are in fact starving but they will not suck and soon become too weak to try. The sound of a whole litter 'gulling' is quite unmistakeable and brings one's nerves almost to breaking point, coupled with the loss of sleep in order to try and save perhaps just one puppy.

Some twenty years ago I experienced this time and again and proved beyond doubt that even if a bitch puppy was saved it in turn would not be able to rear a normal litter owing to the blood being infected through the dam. Very little was known about the disease at the time although it was believed to be connected with virus Hepatitis.

The puppies were sent away for research and the bitches as well as the new born puppies had injections of gamma globulin but with no success. The obvious course was to cut one's losses and breed only from fresh young bitches. With the advent of penicillin and other drugs and inoculation against virus hepatitis it does not seem to be prevalent today and I am thankful to say I have never experienced it since.

GASTRO-ENTERITIS

Diarrhoea of a persistent nature is often accompanied by blood stains. There is also vomiting and the dog is in obvious pain. There will be considerable loss of appetite but the dog should be encouraged to eat milky foods if possible and kept off meat and biscuit meal. Veterinary advice should be sought.

HAEMATOMA

This is a swelling or tumour containing blood and serous fluid. It may occur anywhere on the anatomy but the most usual place is on the inside of the ear flap. It is caused by bruising of the subcutaneous tissues which in all long-eared dogs can come about by continuous shaking of the head. The cause of the irritation is usually canker or lice along the edge of the ear which is the usual place to find them. The swelling appears on the inside of the ear flap and can become very enlarged so that the ear hangs down heavily on one side. It will be very hot and painful.

A simple operation by a veterinary surgeon can be performed to let the fluid out. The wound should not be encouraged to heal too quickly but be allowed to drain for a day or two otherwise the aperture will refill with fluid. All precautions should be taken to remove the cause of the trouble by treating the ear for canker, mange or lice.

HYSTERIA

The animal appears frightened and the eyes staring. He will run wildly about giving a high pitched bark as he goes and banging into anything in his way. The dog should be restrained and put into a darkened room until he has quietened down. Care should be taken that he does not bite anyone handling him as he will not know what he is doing. Unlike epilepsy the animal will make a great deal of noise which can affect other dogs adjacent to him such as at shows, and induce them to behave in an hysterical manner.

The affected dog should be isolated as quickly as possible. The cause of hysteria is often due to worms in puppies or teething troubles, when the gums are swollen and red prior to the molars coming through or when a baby tooth needs removing to allow another one to come through. It can cause excessive pain. An unsuitable diet is another cause of hysteria, or food that is stale or contaminated in some way.

MANGE

There are a great number of skin troubles which come under this heading but only two kinds of mange are of general importance to the dog owner and breeder. They are sarcoptic mange and follicular mange.

Follicular Mange. This type of mange seems to affect the short coated breeds more than dogs such as Golden Retrievers with long coats. It is caused by a mite which burrows into the skin and causes the hair to fall out in small patches. The area will become red and raw from the continual scratching caused by intense irritation. It usually starts on the head, neck and forelegs. Gradually the patches will merge together until in severe cases the dog is almost bare of hair. The skin will thicken and the surface will become dry and scurfy in appearance. The intense irritation will cause the dog to become morose. It is extremely difficult to cure this type of mange but if taken in the early stages there are good proprietary remedies which will help.

Sarcoptic Mange. This is a much more common type of mange and is also caused by a mite which produces intense irritation. It is extremely infectious and care should be taken to burn all bedding and isolate any dog so affected. The mite can be harboured in cracks and crevices particularly in wooden kennels or beds and may lie dormant for several months before becoming active. Old and dusty kennels should be scrubbed and creosoted or a blow lamp used where possible.

It is first noticed on the dog by a pustular spot which eventually breaks and forms a scab. It is quickly brought to the notice of the owner by the continual scratching usually under the forelegs, inner thighs and neck but it will spread to all parts of the body if not brought under control. In the past there have been many remedies such as sulphur baths but modern research has produced many effective skin baths mostly containing Gammexane in which the dog should be bathed every fourth day. After the first two baths it is not usually necessary to saturate the whole of the dog unless it is widespread. The dog should be allowed to dry naturally without any towelling which is very drastic in cold weather. It responds very well to treatment, the skin usually turning grey and it will take some while before the coat will regain its usual gloss as this condition causes it to become dry and staring.

POISONS

In all cases of poisoning veterinary advice should be sought at once, but first aid action should be taken immediately. A piece of common soda pushed down the dog's throat or an emetic of salt and water will help to make him sick. I suppose that rat poison and strychnine are two of the most common types which dogs are liable to pick up, and in the case of strychnine, permanganate of potash may be dissolved in water and poured down the dog's throat as an antidote. It should be done quickly as the effect of strychnine is so rapid that it usually proves fatal.

PYOMETRA

This is a condition which sometimes affects middle aged or elderly bitches. It is an infection of the uterus and if not diagnosed promptly it can have serious results. Bitches which have never had a litter seem to be more prone to it than brood bitches, but this is not always the case. The symptoms are a loss of appetite and a raised temperature coupled with excessive drinking and a swollen abdomen. Frequently there is an evil smelling discharge of pus from the vulva and the bitch seems to be constantly attractive about a month after a season and the behaviour of other dogs will draw one's attention to it. If the uterus remains closed the pus will accumulate and the abdomen become swollen and hard. This is a more dangerous condition than where there is a discharge and usually an operation to remove the uterus will be recommended, whilst in the first case if there is a discharge the veterinary surgeon may try a course of antibiotics before resorting to surgery. After the operation the bitch generally makes a quick recovery. If the bitch has not previously produced a living litter of puppies it will not be possible to show her any more according to Kennel Club rules. If, however, she has registered offspring she can be shown with special permission from the Kennel Club. Unfortunately one of the effects of this operation particularly in a young bitch is that she will put on weight and will be difficult to keep in show condition.

RICKETS

This condition is caused by incorrect feeding and rearing. It is most common in young puppies. The symptoms are enlarged joints and an arched spine. The forelegs will be bowed and the hindlegs very cow hocked. Although it can be improved with treatment the puppies will never really become normal. A balanced diet of eggs, milk, raw meat and biscuit meal is advised with added cod liver oil and calcium.

RINGWORM

This disease can be contracted from close proximity to cattle who may be suffering from it. It can also be transferred to human beings and is very contagious. It is a fungoid disease and needs veterinary treatment. The dog loses its coat in small circles all over its body and will try to alleviate the irritation by continual scratching.

STAPHYLOCOCCAL LYMPHADENITIS

Many will have seen from time to time dogs who are permanently scarred around the muzzle and sometimes round the cheeks and eyes as well. This is caused by a staphylococcal infection in young puppies, and having had it occur on two occasions in the past thirty years I have tried to find the cause and the cure. It is by no means a common ailment, neither is it rare. Possibly owing to increased breeding it seems to be turning up more frequently and more cases are heard of. In recent months I have taken two puppies to Bristol University School of Veterinary Medicine for diagnosis. Although familiar with it, relatively little is known about it, but the following notes were passed to me for publication, in the hope that they will be of some help to any unfortunate breeder who may discover that he has a puppy in his litter showing signs of a staphylococcal infection.

'The condition is seen from time to time in puppies of between six and twelve weeks of age. For reasons which remain obscure it seems to be restricted to a few breeds only, Labradors and Retrievers (both black and golden), Basset Hounds and Spaniels being most prominent.

Presenting symptoms may be listed:

(1) Moist discharge on the inside of the ears which on drying becomes crusty.

(2) Swelling of the local lymph glands. These are located at the inner aspect of the angle of the jaw and also just in front of the shoulder blade. These swellings are painful and may reach one inch in diameter. Occasionally these glands abscessate and rupture discharging a foul-smelling blood-stained pus.

(3) The skin of the face may become pustulated particularly around the nose and eyes.

(4) In extreme cases there may be respiratory involvement.

The cause of the condition is complex. There is little doubt that it is primarily a staphylococcal infection. However, the puppy seems to respond to the infection in a peculiar way in that it develops an allergy to the causative bacteria.

Thus treatment is recommended on three lines:

(a) Antibiotic by injection to control the infection.

(b) Anti-allergic drugs.

(c) Antibiotic/corticosteroid cream applied locally to reduce inflammation and so prevent self-injury to affected areas.

The prognosis for puppies affected by this condition is not good. Although treatment may be successful in so far as the condition is arrested, the face and ears usually remain permanently scarred. Prospective buyers are not attracted to such puppies although by the time they are a year old the scars may be minimal.'

It will have been seen from the above notes that if the condition is recognised at the onset and the correct treatment started at once the chances are favourable that a cure will be effected in which no noticeable scarring will remain.

The puppy does not in himself appear ill, nor does he go off his food, the first signs being the enlarged glands in the neck. The illness seems to extend over a period of three weeks until the glands go down and scabs form on the face where it has pustulated. Once the scabs have come off the hair around has a chance of growing, and it can be helped by bathing in olive oil night and morning.

In many cases the hair will eventually grow again to a large extent, but although some dogs who have suffered from this complaint are seen in the show ring it is doubtful whether they would ever reach top honours, even though they may be excellent in every other way. If discarded as show dogs they can become perfect pets so that it is worth the effort to try and cure them.

STINGS

The most common are bee and wasp stings. In the case of a bee sting, the sting should be removed as quickly as possible. Wasps do not leave their stings behind. Swab immediately with a sting remedy, as used for humans, or with any available spirit, or use bicarbonate of soda or diluted ammonia. If a dog is stung in the mouth or throat, veterinary advice should be sought.

WORMS

There are several types of worm which are common to dogs and these are often the cause of bad condition in puppies and adults. It is as well to be able to identify the type of worm so that the source of the infection can be removed.

Roundworms

These affect puppies from a very early age and in appearance they are like pieces of white string faintly tinged with pink, or they are perhaps more aptly described in likeness to vermicelli. They are found in the intestines in various numbers and in some cases it is quite astonishing the number of worms which can be expelled by one puppy after dosing. The intestines can become completely blocked with worms and sometimes they reach the stomach in which case they are vomited up by the puppy. The symptoms are a distended or 'pot bellied' stomach. The coat is harsh and staring, and the skin dry. Appetite is variable. Some days it is difficult to satisfy them and the next day they will not eat at all. Loose stools are also an indication of worms.

The temperament of a badly infected puppy can be entirely altered when properly wormed. A nervous excitable puppy will become content and relaxed. Convulsions in puppies are usually caused by worms or teething troubles. Briefly the life cycle of a worm takes about eight or nine days from the larva being absorbed into the blood stream until it reaches the lungs and is subsequently coughed up into the windpipe, whereupon it is swallowed and goes back into the intestines to mature into a worm. Hence the necessity of repeating the vermifuge ten days after the first dose. On reaching maturity eggs are passed out of the intestines in the faeces and may stay dormant for months until swallowed by the puppy or other host to begin the life cycle again. It is then that the egg is hatched so to speak and the young larva leaves the digestive tract for the blood stream. When large numbers of larvae are in the lungs at the same time a form of pneumonia is set up and the puppy may become ill and even die. For this reason it will be seen that it is essential that all puppies should be correctly wormed before leaving home. It is also extremely important that the utmost hygiene should be observed in the kennel to be sure that the puppy does not reinfect himself by licking anything on the ground which may be harbouring the eggs of the roundworm. This is one reason why concrete runs are to be recommended as they can be washed down regularly and disinfected.

Tapeworms

There are many different types of tape worm but only two or three are usually found in the dog. It is possible, however, for the dog to be harbouring more than one kind at once.

Unlike the roundworm the tape worm must have an intermediate host such as a louse or flea, rabbit or hare, horse, ox or pig according to the type of tape worm. The body is made up of many segments which grow from the parent head, the youngest segments being next to the head and the oldest and ripest at the tail end. The parent head adheres by hooks or suckers to the wall of the intestine. Although the segments are joined together by hooks they are in fact complete worms in themselves and can lead a separate existence. As the segments ripen they break away and are expelled with the faeces. Each segment contains eggs which are then ready to be swallowed by the intermediate host.

Taenia Cucumerina. is one of the most common which is found in the dog and his host is the louse or flea.

Taenia Serrata. Rabbits and hares form the intermediate host for this type of tape worm. When allowed to eat the entrails the worm quickly germinates in the intestine of the dog.

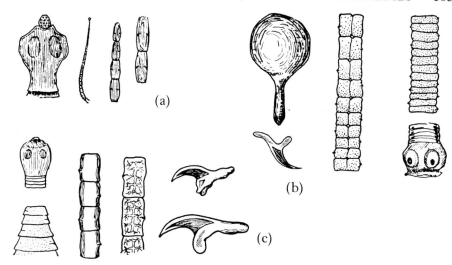

(a) Tapeworm *Taenia Cucumerina* showing head and segments.
(b) Tapeworm *Taenia Marginata* showing head, segments, hook and cyst which is sometimes known as a bladder worm.
(c) Tapeworm *Taenia Serrata* showing head and segments with magnified hooks.

Taenia Marginata. This is the longest type of worm, sometimes reaching six feet in length. Its host is found amongst cattle, sheep and pigs. Uncooked organs from these animals should not be fed to dogs if there is any likelihood of infection.

Hookworms

These are rarely found in dogs in Great Britain but when present can cause severe anaemia, emaciation and general depression, coupled with bloodstained diarrhoea. The worm is about half an inch long with a hook bent backwards just before the head. The body is white. The life cycle is similar to that of the roundworm. It is necessary for the faeces to be examined under a microscope to be sure if there are any eggs from the hookworm present.

Common Remedies

I have always regarded prevention as better than cure. With common sense management many dogs go through their whole lives without a day's illness or the necessity to call in a vet except for early inoculation at about twelve weeks old. It is odd how some people fly to the vet for the least little thing. Often one sells a perfectly healthy pup and the first thing the new owner does is take it to the vet to find out if there is anything wrong with it.

It is usually the owner of the pet dog who spends most time at the veterinary surgeon's surgery, when with a little knowledge of how to deal with simple ailments much unnecessary expense could be avoided. Owners of kennels usually equip themselves with a number of remedies and probably spot any sign of trouble and treat it before it gets out of hand, by keeping a supply of useful medicines.

Your Dog's Medicine Chest

Antiseptic. Dettol, T.C.P. or similar mild antiseptic are excellent for general purposes but Cetavlon is less stringent for bathing cuts and wounds. It is a wise precaution to wipe over the feet and head of a dog at a show with either T.C.P. or Dettol, particularly at indoor shows where infection is so easily picked up.

Boracic powder. A good general stand-by, used dry or as a lotion.

Canker powder. This is essential and should be used regularly if there is any sign of canker, but the occasional dusting is usually sufficient to keep the ears in perfect condition.

Clinical thermometer. This is a most necessary adjunct to any medicine chest. It is best to buy one marked thirty seconds as it requires a shorter time to register. First of all see that the mercury is shaken down to read below about 35°C(98°F). Carefully insert the thermometer into the rectum. On no account should it be forced; a little liquid paraffin smeared on to it will help. Leave the thermometer in place for half a minute and then withdraw and wipe clean with some cotton wool. The normal temperature of a dog varies slightly in different individuals as with human beings but it should be about 38.6°C(101.5°F). Variations in the same dog do occur for no apparent reason, but anything above 38.9°C(102°F) should be regarded as a fever.

After use remember to shake the mercury down and clean and disinfect the thermometer thoroughly before returning it to its case.

Insect powder. For use against all external parasites. Insect repellant collars or strips are an alternative. The collar is suitable for adult dogs and if the instructions issued with it are followed it is most effective. It need only be worn at night. A Vapona strip placed in the kennel will insure against any parasites, but I would not recommend its use where there are puppies, or if the kennel is a very small one, as the vapour may be a bit overpowering for the dog unless there is good ventilation.

Kaolin powder. This is useful to have by you and can be sprinkled on the food in case of loose motions particularly in puppies. It can alternatively be mixed up with some milk, but if the puppies are off their food more drastic measures must be taken, and I always keep a supply of tablets for this purpose, so that if a puppy has diarrhoea and is off his food he can be dosed at once.

Puppies can have diarrhoea for many reasons such as change of diet, too much food or too rich a diet, as well as the more serious disorders which can arise. Prompt action can avoid a lot of trouble and the puppy can be back on his food and fully recovered the next day. Like children they can go up and down very quickly but if neglected serious conditions can result.

Liquid paraffin. Used as an occasional laxative, e.g. at whelping time or if a dog becomes constipated through eating too many bones. Frequent or excessive doses should be avoided.

Milk of magnesia. For all digestive troubles, and can be given to a bitch after whelping should her milk for any reason be too acid.

Penicillin eye ointment. Obtained from your vet, and if kept cool is always useful in case of eye trouble. Inflammation caused by a foreign body or damage to the cornea can be relieved and rapidly cured by the application of a little ointment night and morning. A damaged cornea can be serious if neglected, whereas it can be healed within two or three days if treated at once.

Peroxide of hydrogen. I find this invaluable at the first sign of a patch of wet eczema. Dilute in warm water, using about a dessertspoonful to half a pint of water. Bathe the affected part and if necessary cut off the surrounding hair so that the air can penetrate. Dry thoroughly and dust with boracic powder or dress with calamine lotion. Repeat three times a day, which will prevent the eczema from spreading and will dry it up surprisingly quickly. If neglected this type of eczema can spread alarmingly and professional help will then be necessary.

Potassium permanganate. In case of a dog being bitten by an adder, potassium permanganate crystals rubbed into the wound will act as first aid treatment until the animal can be injected with anti-snake serum.

Skin bath. (See 'Mange')

Travel sickness pills. There are several kinds which can be obtained either from your veterinary surgeon or from a chemist. If a dog is a bad traveller this is usually due to nerves, and once he finds that he can travel without being sick he will get over the trouble completely.

Witch hazel or calamine lotion. This is useful if the skin is irritated and the dog is making things worse by scratching, but more specific treatment may also be needed.

Worming tablets. For round worms in puppies I like to use Coopane, but there are many proprietary makes of worm medicine. Coopane tablets can be obtained from your veterinary surgeon and an adequate supply of these or other tablets should always be kept in hand. They are administered by giving one tablet for every ten pounds body weight, and repeating the dose ten days later.

When you are dosing an adult dog for tape worms seek your vet's advice, particularly if it is for a bitch after she has been mated. No matter what brand of medicine you are using, it is important to give the correct dose to suit the size of the dog it is prescribed for and the dog must be accurately weighed.

Yeast or yeast tablets. Both brewer's yeast and yeast tablets are a great tonic and a quick pick me up if the dog is out of sorts, but they should not be continued indefinitely.

Note:

PARVO VIRUS
Since the last edition of this book most dog owners will know that an additional serious disease now known as parvo virus has reached this country and can be lethal to puppies and older dogs especially, so that early diagnosis is essential.

This is a very virulent virus which can be carried on clothes and shoes and remain dormant for some time in the environment. Symptoms take the form of sickness and diarrhoea with consequent dehydration so that the sufferer needs to be given glucose and water frequently or put on a drip system.

Much research has been done and now fortunately immunisation is available and can be included when the animal is injected for distemper and hard pad, and boosted annually. An additional injection is generally recommended to be given for a bitch prior to being mated or during pregnancy.

8 Hereditary Diseases

In recent years it has become apparent that there have been many cases of Golden Retrievers who have gone blind at an early age.

Dr Keith C. Barnett M.A.Ph.D.B.Sc.M.R.C.V.S. has done and is still doing a great deal of research into hereditary eye diseases.

In 1968 he gave a lecture to members of the Golden Retriever Club in order to help breeders to recognise any eye abnormality and to encourage them to have all their dogs' eyes examined before breeding from them. In the same year the British Veterinary Association took the matter up and inaugurated a scheme by which breeds which are known to suffer from progressive retinal atrophy could be examined by a board of examiners.

This was followed in May 1969 with a scheme to cover hereditary cataract. An intermediate certificate is issued each year until the dog reaches the prescribed age limit when a permanent certificate is given. In each breed this varies. Golden Retrievers may receive a permanent certificate stating that the dog is clear from cataract at three years of age and progressive retinal atrophy at six years of age.

Dr Barnett is of the opinion that if only clear dogs are bred from, the breed could be cleared of hereditary cataract in a matter of two generations as it is caused by a dominant gene.

The following information has been gathered from Dr Barnett's lecture and more recent data, which he has given me as fresh evidence is constantly coming to light.

Cataract

Cataract is an opacity in the lens of the eye and after the examination of the eyes of hundreds of dogs this type of cataract has been found to be inherited in the Golden Retriever.

This form of hereditary cataract differs from any other form which may be caused by injury, diet deficiency or inflammation. It is peculiar to Golden Retrievers and Labradors, though less common in Labradors. One or both eyes may be affected but usually both.

It can be diagnosed by a vet using an ophthalmoscope and can be detected at the early age of six months but more frequently at a year old or later. All significant cases appear before the age of three, and it is advisable to check stud dogs and brood bitches annually until they reach that age.

Transmission is by means of a simple dominant gene. If an affected dog or bitch has not been diagnosed before producing a litter then the cataract may be evident in the offspring, but cataract-free parents do not produce affected puppies. Any clear litter-mates of affected animals cannot act as 'carriers' or transmit the gene to their own offspring.

The gene varies in penetration, and this causes the cataract to vary considerably in size and appearance. A small propeller-shaped cataract at the posterior polar position – i.e., in the centre or back of the lens, will not progress or affect the dog's vision until senile changes of the lens take place, but a dog which has total dense cataract may be blind before the age of two years. These variations bear no relation to the degree in which the offspring may be affected. A bitch with a minute cataract mated to a 'clear' dog may still produce puppies who will be blind at two years old, and the proportion of affected and clear dogs in such a litter is unknown.

It can be appreciated from this description that much thought must be given to the mating of any affected animal, and a very careful examination and selection of the progeny must be made if a cataract-free line is to be established. To free the breed from hereditary cataract all stud dogs and brood bitches should have their eyes examined before breeding and no affected animal should be bred from. By this method the Golden Retriever breed could be cleared of hereditary cataract in one or two generations.

Progressive Retinal Atrophy

Progressive retinal atrophy is inherited in many breeds of dogs, as well as in humans, and laboratory animals. For diagnosis the retina is examined with an ophthalmoscope. Early cases can only be diagnosed by a veterinary surgeon experienced in eye diseases. The symptoms are the narrowing of the blood vessels of the eye and the presence of pigment spots on the retina. Cases can develop in a matter of a few months in dogs who have apparently good sight, but in others there is a more gradual approach to total blindness.

The disease does not develop in Golden Retrievers until later than in other breeds where it is sometimes seen as early as three months old.

In Labradors and Border Collies, where it has been a major problem, it usually develops by the time they are two years old.

It should not be assumed, as is sometimes suggested, that any dog whose eyes have a particularly deep glow has progressive retinal atrophy as this is not so.

Unlike the progressive retinal atrophy found in some breeds where the outer part of the retina is first affected, progressive retinal atrophy in

Golden Retrievers first attacks the centre of the retina while the outer part is still clear. This explains why Goldens may be worked until quite badly affected, as they can see moving objects to left or right but not directly in front of them.

Research is being done at Cambridge to establish the earliest age at which progressive retinal atrophy can be diagnosed, by specially breeding dogs in which it is likely to develop. In these circumstances, the earliest age at which Dr Barnett has found it is at three months old. Breeders, however, must not wait until all the answers are found before trying to eliminate the disease.

The following is the procedure to be followed in Britain when an owner wishes to have his dog certified as free from P.R.A. and hereditary cataract.

1. The owner takes the dog to his own veterinary surgeon and requests that the animal be examined with a view to the issue of a certificate.
2. The veterinary surgeon examines the dog and if there is, in his opinion, nothing to prevent the dog going forward, suggests a referee from a list provided, reminding the owner to take with him to the referee the dog's Kennel Club registration certificate and any related transfer certificate(s).
3. The owner then gets in touch with the referee, saying that he has been referred by his veterinary surgeon. He then takes the dog to the referee, with the certificates mentioned in Note 2 above.
4. The referee examines the dog and signs the report. He gives one copy to the owner, keeps one for himself, and sends the third copy to the B.V.A.
5. The owner then sends the report to the Kennel Club, requesting a certificate of freedom from P.R.A. and hereditary cataract.
6. If the report is favourable, the Kennel Club will issue a permanent or interim certificate as the case may be.

BREEDS IN WHICH P.R.A. IS KNOWN TO BE A PROBLEM

Welsh Corgi (Cardigan)	3 years
Welsh Corgi (Pembroke)	4 years
Collie (Rough)	3 years
Dachshund (Smooth-Haired)	5 years
Dachshund Miniature (Long-haired)	3 years
Elkhound	3 years
Retriever (Labrador)	4 years
Poodle (Miniature)	5 years
Poodle (Toy)	5 years
Retriever (Golden)	6 years
Saluki	3 years

Shetland Sheepdog	3 years
Spaniel (Cocker)	5 years
Spaniel (Springer, English)	5 years
Tibetan Terriers	3 years
Other Breeds	5 years

Entropion and Trichiasis

It is usually possible to diagnose these conditions when the puppies are still young. Symptoms can become noticeable whilst they are being weaned, or later when they are teething. Occasionally these conditions develop in older puppies but generally before they are a year old.

One or both eyes may be affected. The eye weeps continously, and this is the only one of the three eye conditions affecting Golden Retrievers which is actually painful to the dog. In bad cases the result can be erosion of the cornea.

An operation is needed to bring relief, but this is a simple one, and when it has been carried out there is no further trouble, nor should there be any scarring if done expertly.

However, the conditions referred to are inherited and dogs and bitches who have been affected should not be bred from if a clear strain is to be established.

Hip Dysplasia

I am greatly indebted to the British Veterinary Association for the following information and line drawings on hip dysplasia which I am sure will be of great benefit to all those who are anxious to eradicate all evidence of hip abnormality from the breed.

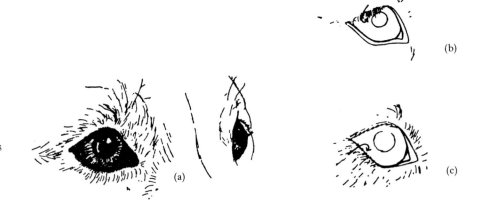

(a)   Normal eye.
(b)   Trichiasis, upper eyelid;
(c)   Entropion, lower eyelid; in (b) and (c) the eyelashes are rubbing against the surface of the eyeball.

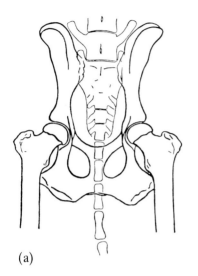

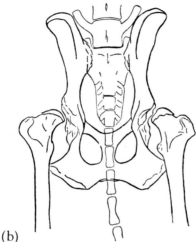

(a)

(b)

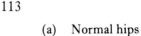

(a)   Normal hips
(b)   Hip dysplasia

WHAT YOU SHOULD KNOW ABOUT HIP DYSPLASIA

What Is Hip Dysplasia?

Dysplasia means abnormal development or growth, thus hip dysplasia results in badly shaped hips. It occurs in both man and animals, but is particularly troublesome in some breeds of dog.

The hip joint is a ball and socket joint, the ball being the head of the femur and the socket the acetabulum of the pelvic bone. In the normal hip the ball is smooth and round, and fits snugly into the socket. When a puppy is born the bones are relatively soft, but as they grow changes can take place so that the socket becomes shallow and the ball becomes distorted. As the animal gets older and heavier further changes can take place so that the dog may become lame and unable to move without pain.

Severe cases are readily recognised clinically from a very early age, but unless detected by X-ray examination, the less severe cases can pass unnoticed until the dog eventually goes unsound or his working ability is impaired.

What Are The Causes Of Hip Dysplasia?

Hip Dysplasia occurs most commonly in dogs of the larger breeds. It is known that the disease is inherited. It is most likely that the genetic factors involved produce one or more of the following: insufficient pelvic muscle; failure of the head of the femur in the socket to develop properly; faulty angulation between the pelvis and the femur. In fat and over heavy bodied puppies, the condition is aggravated.

There is considerable evidence that by following a careful breeding programme, using normal animals, it is possible to reduce the number of cases in each breed.

How Can Hip Dysplasia Be Eradicated?

It must be realised that only after some considerable time can this widespread condition finally be eradicated from some breeds of dog. An essential start is to breed where possible from normal animals and to out cross as much as possible, preferably to strains known to be free of hip dysplasia.

How Can We Recognise The Disease?

The British Veterinary Association in collaboration with the Kennel Club, has a scheme for the control of hip dysplasia. This scheme has been specially designed to help dog breeders of those breeds where the condition is a problem or likely to become a problem, to select their breeding stock so as to minimise the possibility of producing dysplastic pups. This scheme can also be usefully applied to other breeds.

Under the scheme, animals over one year old, and under six years old are X-rayed by a veterinary surgeon, who submits the radiographs which are considered to approach normality, to a specialist panel of veterinary surgeons who have made a particular study of interpreting the films.

A full and detailed report is produced and if the dog shows no evidence of abnormality a certificate is issued by the Kennel Club. In certain cases where there are only slight deviations from the normal the breeder is informed, so that until he breeds a normal dog he may prefer to use this animal rather than another which has greater hip abnormalities, or other undesirable features.

It would be most unwise to breed from a dog which showed hip dysplasia to any marked degree. Where possible only dogs which show no evidence of hip dysplasia should be used for breeding.

It will be seen how necessary it is for all persons intending to breed a litter to have both the sire and dam X-rayed. It must be emphasised that once the film has been considered normal by one's own veterinary surgeon it should be submitted to a specialist panel who have made a particular study of this condition. A positive diagnosis of hip dysplasia can only be made radiographically. It is essential that the X-ray plates are of the highest quality, particularly in those cases where there may be only the slightest deviations from normal.

Scrutineers will disregard any plates in which the dog has been incorrectly positioned, or which are not of a sufficiently high standard to enable a diagnosis to be made.

Dogs of under one year or over six years of age will not be accepted under the British Veterinary Association Scheme.

X-Ray Procedure

In many cases a short-acting general anaesthetic or tranquilliser will be necessary to position the dog satisfactorily although most Golden Retrievers are extremely well behaved and I have never found this necessary myself. Some veterinary surgeons insist that the dog is anaesthetized in order to relax the limbs whilst others do not.

The dog is placed on his back with his pelvis centred over the cassette and his chest is supported by a cradle. The hind legs are pulled straight back, completely extending all the hind-limb joints. It is essential that the body of the dog does not roll to one side. This may be prevented by extending the forelegs and tying each to a corner of the table or they can be extended and held in position.

The date of birth and the Kennel Club Registration Certificate number must be photographed on the plate at the time that it is exposed. If the plates come within the standards of normality a certificate will be issued which must be sent to the Kennel Club.

9 Training and Working

Training

Not everyone can give a Golden Retriever the chance to show his prowess in the field, but if possible every owner should do something to educate his dog to make him into an amiable and obedient member of the household or kennel.

The success of your training depends not only on your ability to teach the puppy but also on the correct temperament and character of the puppy himself. Some puppies show signs of natural ability from a very early age and will pick up all sorts of objects and carry them around with great pleasure. The puppy should be encouraged to bring whatever he is carrying to you and praised for doing so, but do not enter into a game if he decides to go off in the opposite direction. At this age he is better ignored as the day will come later when serious training must begin and it is better that he should know nothing at all rather than have learnt a bad habit at an early age. Many good dogs are ruined by bad handling, and more often than not the seeds of bad behaviour are sown when the puppy is very young.

Most Golden Retrievers are intelligent and have a natural desire to please, and love the work they were bred for. If you have decided that you are going to train your dog to the gun the basic training is the same whether or not you wish later to go on to Working Tests or Field Trials.

It is most important that the would-be trainer and owner should know exactly what he should expect from his dog. Apart from knowing that he is a gun dog many people have no idea what kind of work he is intended to do.

A Retriever is bred to hunt and bring to hand dead and wounded game. It is not primarily his job to flush live game as this is a spaniel's work, but many retriever owners who have some rough shooting require this of them. In this case only an older dog should be allowed to hunt if he is to remain steady. Once a young dog has been permitted to flush birds it will be extremely difficult to keep him under control when working on shot birds, and in any case the basic training must be done thoroughly first of all.

Many owners do not understand the difference between the work of Retrievers and that of Setters and Pointers, who work entirely by scent in the air and not on the ground as in the case of Retrievers and Spaniels. The work which Setters and Pointers do is to scent live unshot birds from as far away as possible without flushing them until the gun is in position. When the birds are flushed and shot it is then the Retrievers's job to retrieve them from where they have fallen and deliver them to hand. As a rule, Setters and Pointers do not retrieve, but their work is extremely fascinating to watch and is a highly skilled operation when correctly carried out.

Many times I have been told by people who own retrievers that their dogs bring articles to them but will not put them down. In their ignorance they expect the object to be laid at their feet, whereas in fact the dog is doing exactly what he is supposed to do, 'bringing to hand', and he should be encouraged to release into your hand whatever he has brought and never put it down.

How often one sees dogs being exercised by someone throwing either a stick, stone or ball for the dog to go rushing after and bring back. Never do this with a retriever, even in the early days, if you intend to train him at a later date. In any case stones can damage the teeth, and bouncing balls are highly dangerous. I know of one Golden Retriever Champion who died through being choked in this way.

EQUIPMENT FOR TRAINING

First you will require a good loud whistle of the rather shrill type which the dog can hear even if he is hunting in kale or roots. The noise of his tail beating about the wet leaves makes it very difficult for him to hear you and in all probability he will not be able to see you either. The human whistle is not penetrating enough.

Teach your puppy to come immediately, when he hears a few short blasts on the whistle. If in the early days you are training him to come to a whistle and he stops at some distance and looks at you, but does not come because he does not understand what you require of him, crouch low to the ground and continue to blow short sharp notes on the whistle. It always seems to intrigue puppies to see humans looking like dogs and they come at once to investigate. Once he understands what the whistle means this of course will not be necessary.

He should also learn the word 'come' used in conjunction with the whistle. Always insist that he does come when you call him and never call him back unless you really mean it. Do not let him get away with half measures.

When punishment is necessary through deliberate disobedience then it is better to take him by the scruff of the neck and shake him, scolding at the same time, rather than resort to a beating.

Dummies

These can be made in various ways and need not be elaborate. To begin training a puppy a sock filled with nylon stockings is as good as anything as it is both light and soft. On no account should a heavy or hard dummy be used. A plastic detergent container is excellent for size so long as it is well padded and not filled with anything too heavy. I usually keep one dummy with a rabbit or hare skin wrapped round it or a pair of duck's wings attached by means of an elastic band to make the dummy more realistic.

You will also need a dummy for use in water and the best type to have is a cork-filled one which is both light and buoyant. These can be bought ready made from some gunsmiths. Canvas dummies are frequently used but are inclined to be too heavy for a young puppy.

Equip yourself with at least three dummies for land and two for use in water.

Leads

One more thing which you must have is a slip lead. These can be obtained from most good pet stores but can be made quite easily and effectively from nylon rope. Cut the rope to the length you require and seal each end by burning it. Buy a small ring about an inch across. These are easily obtained at a hardware shop. Attach the ring to the cord. For a few pence a shoe mender or saddler will make a very neat job of it for you. You can also have a loop made the other end if you wish. Now thread the rope through the ring and adjust it to fit your dog by putting a knot either side of the ring.

I have found these leads most useful and they are light and easily put into one's pocket as well as being cheap and easy to make.

THE STARTING PISTOL AND DUMMY THROWER

When the puppy is sufficiently advanced in his training it will be necessary to accustom him to gunfire and for this purpose a starter pistol is less alarming than a shotgun. Walk some distance from the dog before you throw the dummy and fire at it with your pistol. He will soon connect the two things when he sees the dummy thrown up in the air and immediately hears the bang. Once he has got used to this you will have no problems when it comes to the real thing.

Sometimes a puppy is gun nervous rather than gun-shy. In this case he will do his retrieve correctly, then probably try and creep away. A gun-shy dog will immediately run away as soon as the gun is fired. Generally speaking a gun-nervous dog will get over it with age and experience.

Dummy throwers are most useful for the average dog but some puppies are apprehensive of them at first. They do not like the rather hollow sound they make and in this case it is better to stick to a starter pistol until they have gained more confidence. But for the single-handed trainer the dummy thrower is a boon as the dummy is thrown a great distance and the dog can be made to mark his bird when he hears the bang.

Training Your Puppy

First and foremost owner and dog must have complete confidence in each other. It is no good to start out for a lesson if you are already irritated with the dog as you will quickly lose patience with him and more harm will be done than good.

He must be taught to 'sit' on command or as soon as the hand is raised with the palm downwards indicating the sit position. If necessary press him down firmly on the rump repeating the word 'sit'. Some people use the word 'drop' but this is more usually applicable to Spaniels.

To teach him to walk to heel, start with him on a slack lead repeating the word 'heel' and slapping the side of your leg to show him where to walk.

It is useful if you have a narrow pathway with a hedge or wall beside it so that the dog has to walk close beside you. If he is co-operating well, slip the lead off and continue walking with him at heel. Periodically stop and make him sit. Insist that he sits immediately.

Most Goldens are excellent retrievers so you should have no trouble in getting him to pick up a thrown dummy. If he does not take to it at first, put it in his mouth and hold it there for a second or two until he gets used to the feel of it. Never let him fetch it until told to do so.

At first you will have to hold him until you have taught him to be steady and wait for the command. Stand in front of him with the hand raised and repeat the word 'stay' after first telling him to sit.

It is best to take the dog away from the vicinity of the kennels as a puppy will often try to take the dummy back to his kennel.

As soon as he has picked it up turn and run away calling him after you. This is to encourage him to come as fast as possible. When he is alongside you, stoop down and take it from him with your right hand coming up under his mouth. Do not drag it out of his mouth from a vertical position.

It is important that he should learn to lift his head up and upon the word 'dead' release the dummy gently into your hand.

The next lesson is to teach him to stay in the sitting position whilst you walk away. Sit the dog down, then take a few paces backwards with the hand raised, saying 'stay'. If he has remained sitting then walk back to him and make a fuss of him to let him know that you are pleased.

If he moves and comes towards you take him right back to the spot he was in and sit him down again. Repeat this several times if necessary.

If he has learnt these three lessons thoroughly by giving him ten to fifteen minutes daily it is a good idea to give them a rest for a few days and let them sink in. When you take him out again go through the usual routine. If he has remembered it you can feel confident in taking him a step further. This time walk a little further away from him and drop one of the dummies close beside you, at the same time holding up your hand and saying 'No'. Pick the dummy up yourself and repeat it several times on either side of you. If the dog makes any attempt to move shout 'No' at him and take him back to his sitting position.

When you are absolutely confident that he has grasped this lesson you can then begin to throw the dummy up in the air further away from you but still continue to pick it up yourself. The next time you take him out it will give you tremendous satisfaction if he goes through all the exercises perfectly and you really will feel that you are getting somewhere particularly if you are on good terms with the dog and he is keen to learn.

The next time you throw the dummy, instead of picking it up go and stand by your dog. Do not make a fuss of him yet. Wait a moment or two then lunge forward pointing in the direction of the dummy saying, 'Hi lost'. Do not be vague about your directions. Once you have got him steady there are endless variations on dummy throwing which you can try out on him so that the lessons never become dull. Do not attempt to do too much or let the lesson last too long. Far more harm is done this way and as I have said a few days' rest to let things he has learnt mature in his mind is a very good thing and he will come out all the fresher and keen to learn the next time.

Having got your dog steady and retrieving to hand the next step is to be able to stop him with the whistle and make him sit. A long drawn out blast is generally used, or some people prefer to use a whistle with a different tone especially for this purpose. The object of this whistle is to make the dog stop and look at its handler in order to take fresh directions. If the dog is at all likely to chase a hare or rabbit which gets up under his nose, the instant whistle and command to sit will make him realise at once that he is still under control even though he is away from your side. This lesson takes time and patience but is quite invaluable in the shooting field. Practise stopping him on all sorts of occasions when he is least expecting it so that he learns to sit automatically as soon as he hears the whistle.

The next step will be to teach him to take directions and this is done by throwing out two dummies and sending him for each in turn. He will probably want to fetch the one thrown last first of all but this must be stopped immediately by blowing the stop whistle. On no account let him pick up the wrong dummy. He must pick up the one you are directing him to. Finally you will be able to throw out three dummies, one either side and one in the middle. Throw them wide apart and give him a clear direction as to which one to fetch. If he makes the slightest attempt to go in the wrong direction blow the stop whistle at once and indicate clearly with your arm pointing in the right direction.

Begin now to throw the dummy into cover, over hedges and into ditches to make it more difficult. It is also a good plan to throw the dummy casually as you are walking along with the dog at heel and having walked a considerable distance send him back for it. Train his memory by increasing the distance. Introduce the puppy to the use of the starting pistol by firing it some distance from him. If he takes to it well then you can advance to the use of the dummy thrower as this will teach the dog to mark the fall and get him used to hunting further away, the distance and the flight of the dummy corresponding more to that of a bird in flight than a hand thrown dummy.

RETRIEVING FROM WATER

If the weather is reasonably warm the puppy may be taught to swim but do not attempt this in the middle of the winter if the puppy is young. The easiest way of teaching him is to allow him to play with other dogs who are good swimmers and he will quickly want to join in. When he has gained confidence then the serious business of retrieving can be begun. Let him see other dogs retrieving and then throw the dummy a short distance but just out of his depth. Once he has actually got his feet off the ground is the moment when he must be encouraged to swim ahead and fetch the dummy. Give him plenty of praise when he comes back with it but walk away when he reaches the bank and call him to you so as to avoid giving him the chance to put the dummy down and shake himself.

This is a bad fault which is easier to stop in the first place than to correct at a later date, so call him urgently to you as you walk away. Most Goldens enjoy the water immensely once they have learnt to swim and when they have really got used to retrieving well from open water the retrieves can be made more difficult, such as hunting in undergrowth after crossing a stretch of water, possibly on an island or opposite bank of a river. Then a decoy dummy can be thrown out when the dog is already swimming. These exercises need skilful training but with an intelligent and keen dog coupled with a patient handler much can be achieved.

One word of warning about sending a dog into water. Do not leave a choke chain or collar on the dog. In the action of swimming the dog's foreleg comes up under the dog's chin and it is the easiest thing in the world for the dog to get his leg through the chain or collar if it is slack.

This has been known to happen and the dog turns over and is drowned before you can do anything about it.

All the exercises previously mentioned are of a nature which will be required if you intend to compete in Working Tests, and if you are more ambitious and want to run your dog in Field Trials the same rules apply but you will need to put them into practice in the shooting field.

If you have perfected your dummy training and you feel that your dog can now advance to the real thing, if possible start with a dead partridge as they are easy to pick up and dogs like them. Throw it as you would a dummy into long grass or stubble and send your dog to retrieve it. He will probably do it without any trouble and once he has got the idea of picking up birds the rest will come easily.

He may not pick up a pheasant very tidily at first. Some dogs are apt to catch hold of one wing in their excitement but this is lack of experience. To teach him to pick it up properly use a dead bird and tie the wings to the body or slip a rubber band over the wings and body.

Throw the bird several times and he will soon get the knack of

A good water entry by Field Trial Ch. Holway Chanter. Owned and handled by Mrs June Atkinson.

rolling the bird over to pick it up correctly. It is very important that he should learn this at once otherwise he will get into the habit of lifting a bird in any fashion and have to put it down several times on the way back because it is either slipping out of his mouth or he cannot see where he is going because he is blinded by a wing across his face.

It is worth spending a little time on this exercise even if you use a cold bird, rather than one freshly shot.

Dogs do not care a lot for pigeons but if they have their wings tied down they can be used in the place of dummies. In this way the feathers do not come out in the dog's mouth when retrieved, which is what a young dog does not like about them.

This chapter is intended to try to help those who wish to give their dog some training but have not much opportunity or facilities for doing so. Much can be achieved in a small garden or even a public park and a great deal of pleasure and satisfaction can be derived from training your own dog. If you live near enough to be able to join a training class then by all means do so as it is only when you take your dog out in company that you can see how good your training has been.

They behave so differently when in company with other dogs than they do on their home ground. If you follow the exercises given in this chapter you should be able to train your puppy to become a useful game-finding dog, one who will hunt freely but always under control.

Whether you are using your dog for rough shooting or picking up at a shoot, be selective about the birds you allow him to pick. Be sure whilst he is still inexperienced that the birds are dead as a flapping pheasant will put a young dog off completely and he may become afraid to pick up a bird. Do not allow him to retrieve a hare or rabbit the first season as nothing excites a dog more than a hare getting up and running. Once a dog starts to chase a hare it is most difficult to stop him and often not possible to correct him as you would wish if you are at a shoot. This is a terrible transgression so better to be safe than sorry and keep him strictly on birds until you can rely on his steadiness.

There are several other major sins which must be guarded against, such as unsteadiness, hard mouth, whining or barking and being out of control. Any one of these would put your dog straight out of any competition. There is no reprieve for a dog who runs in even if it is only a few yards and is stopped. It is safest to keep your hands either in your pocket or behind your back but never unconsciously wave them about as a keen dog may genuinely mistake it for a signal to go. I once learnt this to my cost at a trial when I drew a handkerchief from my pocket with a flourish and away went my dog.

Golden Retrievers as a breed are seldom hard mouthed, but sometimes a very keen young dog may grab at a bird which with more experience he would pick more carefully.

WHINING AND BARKING

Here again I think that more Labradors are faulted for this than Golden Retrievers. This is a most annoying habit and one that is almost impossible to cure. I have known several otherwise good dogs who have been a menace at a shoot and useless for competition. Unfortunately it is very catching so try to avoid standing near a whiner, or your own dog may pick up the habit.

A dog out of control at a Trial can be put out of the stake if he is seen by two judges to be flushing unshot game and not responding to his owner's command. If a dog picks up the scent of live game when sent for a dead bird or is seen to be going well away from the expected area hunting up live game and perhaps getting on to the line of a hare then the owner can be told to call his dog up. Nothing can be more embarrassing than for the dog to become suddenly deaf.

Luck plays a large part in Trials as it is impossible for each dog to have the same test. Some dogs get all the easy birds and others get the more difficult ones, but a successful difficult retrieve counts more in the end than a simple one.

The Golden Retriever is happy to work under all kinds of conditions whether he is required to retrieve from thick scrub, brambles, or water. His heavy coat which all Goldens should have together with a thick undercoat protects him and makes him particularly suitable as an all-round gun dog.

There are several books which cover the ground of training thoroughly and I would recommend P.R.A. Moxon's *Gundogs, Training, and Field Trials.*

Field Trials

Field Trials in this country are run on the principle of an ordinary day's shoot.

For those who are not familiar with this procedure a little explanation may be necessary but I do not intend to go into all the technicalities of running and judging a Field Trial. The following paragraphs are intended to help those who have never seen a Field Trial or even been present at a day's shoot to understand what is required of the dog and how a shoot is organised.

With the high cost of rearing pheasants and the general upkeep of large estates where game is preserved, it is not easy to find owners who are willing to give ground for this purpose and each year it becomes more difficult.

Strangely enough interest in training dogs for Field Trials increases and the ground is less easy to acquire. It is for this reason that working tests which are run on dummies or cold game tests are becoming very much more popular.

When a host generously consents to a club running a trial on his ground he is usually a sportsman who is interested in gun dog work himself.

He will choose the date and invite the guns and his head keeper will organise the shoot. This means selecting the ground to be shot over and ensuring that there are sufficient birds available to make an interesting day for everyone. He will arrange all the details in this respect and hire as many beaters as he needs. These are paid for by the club running the trial.

The number of dogs taking part varies between twelve, fifteen or twenty-four. In the latter case the trial is spread over two days. There are several different categories such as Puppy and Novice, Non-Winners and All Aged.

There are always many more applicants than there are places available. A ballot takes place about a week before the trial and each dog is drawn with a number so that the first ones out of the hat are the ones who are given the opportunity to run their dog if they wish. Sometimes it is not convenient as the dog may be ill or in the case of a bitch she may have come in season in which case she would not be eligible. In this event the next name on the list of reserve nominations is offered a place.

The meet usually takes place about 9.30 a.m. The party proceed to the fields or woods as the case may be and assuming that the birds are to be walked up the party spread out in a long line consisting of three judges and usually eight guns together with the beaters and judges' steward, competitors' steward and board holders. These are people who hold up the number of the dog working so that the spectators can identify it. Each judge has with him a handler and a dog on either side of him so that there are six dogs in the line at once. The spectators and dogs not wanted in the line stand either at the end of the line or at some vantage point where they can see what is going on. They have a steward with them holding a red flag and no one must go further forward than the flag as a safety precaution. As the line of people moves forward the birds rise and are shot. If there are hares and rabbits these are shot as well.

The dogs with the judge nearest the guns who shot the birds are sent to retrieve them but the judge must send the lower number of his two dogs first. Should he fail to find it the other dog is sent to try and recover it and if successful scores over the first dog with what is called an 'eye wipe'. In the case of an Open Stake a failure of this nature would be sufficient to put him out of the running altogether.

Each dog is entitled to two retrieves under two judges unless he has been put out of the stake for either 'running in', hard mouth, whining or being out of control.

Very often the birds are driven, depending on the time of the season and the suitability of the ground. Usually in woods the beaters circle the area and drive the game towards the guns. In this case the guns are placed at stands around the outside of the wood and they shoot the birds as they come over. The same procedure takes place, with the judge and two dogs standing near the guns. As the birds fall the dogs mark where they fall and at the end of the drive they are sent in turn to pick them up. Birds which are thought to be runners are retrieved first.

All dogs have to be taken off the lead as soon as they go into the line and come under judge's orders.

The party proceeds from stand to stand. Generally there are four in the morning and three or four in the afternoon. Owing to Field Trial procedure there is bound to be some delay trying out the dogs so that fewer birds are shot than would be on a normal day's shooting, the main aim being to give each dog a fair trial. It is usual for a water retrieve to be arranged at an Open Stake so that each dog has a thorough testing. Those dogs who have done well on all their retrieves will be called back into the line for additional retrieves, and a dog who has excelled on a difficult retrieve will gain more merit.

At the end of the trial the results will be announced. As well as the first four places the judges usually award Certificates of Merit to dogs who have worked well throughout the day and have made no major mistakes, but perhaps have not had quite the style or speed of those placed in the awards.

Working Tests and Other Forms of Training

Working tests provide excellent competition during the closed season when there is no actual work to keep gun dogs in training. They are usually held at week-ends, and many people make it a family day out with a picnic luncheon in pleasant country surroundings.

The tests are run on much the same lines as a Field Trial. These take the form of three or four exercises which have previously been arranged by the organisers to resemble as closely as possible retrieves which are likely to occur during a shooting day.

Tests are scheduled for Puppies and Novices, Non-Winners, and Open Dogs, and the exercises are graded in severity according to the qualification. Puppies are required to walk in line whilst a gun is fired and dummies thrown. For the stiffer grades these may also be thrown into cover or over water, or may be unseen retrieves, which means that the dummies have been placed in position without the dog knowing where, so that he has to rely on his handler to direct him. Sometimes a decoy is used, or the dog may be required to jump over a fence.

Water picnics are also popular in the summer time. These take place by a lake-side, and all the retrieves are centred around the lake. The dummies may be thrown some considerable distance out into the water by a person hiding in the bushes on the bank, or the dummy may be thrown on to an island or promontory so that the dog has to cross the water before hunting for it.

In recent years gun dog tests have become so popular that some Agricultural Societies now stage these events at their shows, and Hunt Committees include them with their Agricultural Sports Day. There is no doubt that gun dog tests are gaining momentum and more people are training their own dogs.

Field Trial Ch. Holway Chanter delivering to hand at the area finals of the U.R.C. working test, 1979.

International Champion Mandingo Buidhe Colum. Owned by the Author. Sire Alresford Nice Fella, ex Alresford Buidhe Derg.

Obedience training has also become extraordinarily popular amongst people who own breeds of all kinds. There is scarcely a town of any size these days which does not have its Dog Training Society, and competitions are held in conjunction with most dog shows where space will permit. Even Charity Exemption Shows now schedule obedience competitions which are excellent for the beginner with a young dog.

More people are beginning to realise their responsibility when purchasing a dog, and the benefit of owning a well behaved one. A gun dog is all the happier for some form of training, even though he may not be used for shooting. In mentioning the opportunities open to him, one must not overlook the work done by the Guide Dogs for the Blind Association, and the splendid record of these dogs, many of them Golden Retrievers, all over the country and in fact all over the world. Their lives are spent in constant devotion to their blind master or mistress, helping to make it a fuller and happier existence and giving them back their independence.

The following story is an example of the initiative of Goldens. Like most dogs they love snow, but in this country, especially in the West Country where I live, it is not often that our dogs can really enjoy it. However, during the last two hard winters we have been cut off by the snow and many sheep have been lost.

At the beginning of the year a local farmer spent many hours digging out his sheep and Jason, who belongs to friends of mine, helped in the rescue. Several days later he was exploring on his own in a different area when his excited barks were heard across the snow. When his owner reached him he was digging furiously and finally uncovered a completely exhausted and almost dead sheep. It is not surprising that Jason became a local hero overnight.

10 Golden Retrievers Abroad

Many people do not realise how far the cult of dog breeding extends and are surprised to learn that dog shows are held in many far away countries such as Pakistan, Ceylon, the Argentine, Brazil, Bermuda, South Africa, Finland, the West Indies, and Australia, to name but a few. Golden Retrievers have been exported to all these countries and many more.

Strangely enough those countries nearer to us do not seem to have adopted them with the same amount of enthusiasm. Although from time to time Goldens have been exported to France they do not seem to have been taken up by any breeders. Nor does one hear of them being bred in Spain or Portugal, although I sent two to an American living in Spain and he bred a litter from them. In Italy too there are many big dog shows and keen breeders, but no one has yet popularised the Golden Retriever there. In Switzerland the breed is better known and a number of Goldens have been exported there in recent years.

Breeding is limited as they have very strict rules which prevent indiscriminate breeding. No bitch can be bred from under two years of age and both dog and bitch must have passed the temperament test preferably in the first twelve months. Each must have a full complement of teeth and a correct bite and must have had its hips X-rayed and found to be satisfactory.

The temperament test is more appropriate for a guard dog than a gun dog. It requires that the owner and dog shall be present on a stipulated day when judges appointed by the Spaniel and Retriever Club assemble in a wood. Here the owner has to walk with the dog who must not show any fear when obstacles such as car tyres are thrown out of trees and blankets shaken in front of it. The dog must also walk on to a railway platform and follow its master into a telephone kiosk. It must also stay steady when encircled by strangers whilst the owner is out of sight.

Such a stringent test means that few litters are bred, and if the bitch has more than eight puppies the authorities insist that the remainder be put down.

Similar rules apply in Germany where there have been a few imports but very little breeding has been done.

Holland seems to be the only European country other than

Scandinavia which has really taken an interest in the breed. In 1956 they founded their own Golden Retriever Club and this has since made great progress. The breed's popularity owes much no doubt to the fact that Her Royal Highness Princess Beatrix fell in love with them and has now a Golden Retriever of her own.

Goldens in Scandinavia

Sh. Ch. Country Boy's Caramel. By N.U. Ch. Caliph of Yeo ex Kirstina of Kuldana. Owned by Mrs Ylva Braunerhjelm.

In recent years, as in every other country where they are bred, Goldens have grown in popularity throughout Scandinavia, especially in Denmark. Here they have a flourishing club called the 'Dansk Retriever Klub' which caters for all five of the Retriever breeds.

Not only do they run their own shows but they organise Field Trials as well. There is a tremendous enthusiasm amongst the Golden Retriever Breeders and in the last ten years they have imported from

this country about eighty Goldens. It is interesting to note that sound hips are of paramount importance and all dogs must be passed clear before their progeny can be registered.

Their stock is almost entirely of English origin although I believe there have been a few importations from Germany and Holland.

I had the pleasure of judging Golden Retrievers at the Dansk Retriever Klub show in 1970 which was held at Valdemars Slot, the lovely home of the Chairman Lensbaron luel-Brockdorff who lavishly entertained all three English judges together with Her Royal Highness Princess Benedikte and her husband Prince Richard who is President of the Club.

The British Ambassador and his wife were also guests and a great interest was shown by everyone both at the show and on the following day at the Field Trials. The latter were run on similar lines to a cold game test in this country. Many dogs were discarded for unsteadiness as live game was used as a distraction. The method of judging both at the Field Trials and the show was somewhat different from our own. The class, which may contain as many as twenty dogs, has to be graded into first, second, and third grade. Only the first grade dogs come back into the ring for a final appraisal and placing. The classification is also different, there being only three classes for each sex. The first class is for young dogs under a year old. This is followed by the Open Class and then the Champion class. It does not seem an arduous classification but each dog has to have a written critique and as there were over seventy Golden Retrievers entered it was quite a task. Although an interpreter was on hand it took quite a time as every word had to be translated and written down. The report does not necessarily have to be lengthy but it is avidly read. I found this rather a cumbersome method and feel that it would be better confined to the first grade dogs only, as it means that not only are the dogs in the ring for a very long while but it becomes rather tiring for the public who tend to lose interest. However, this is the method adopted by all Scandinavian countries.

Norway and Sweden have also imported a number of Goldens from Britain and the number of registered Goldens in these two countries is rapidly increasing. Opportunity for working Goldens is somewhat limited in Norway as they do not have pheasants such as they have in Sweden, but there is an abundance of wild fowl. However the country on the whole is more suited to Setters which are worked in the mountains.

Goldens have been put to other uses and are trained to 'pack carry' which they enjoy. Norwegians are very enthusiastic fishermen and many go on fishing weekends to the mountain-rivers and take their dogs with them to carry all their tackle and tent. Some people have

Int. Nord. U. Ch.
and Nord. L. Ch.
Hedetorpets Morris
and his daughter S.
Sf. U. Ch. Gul-
lhaugens Golden
Caddie. Note the
Swedish type sleigh
harness. Owned by
Margaret and Sigurd
Pekkari, Sweden.

holiday cabins in the more remote areas. Goldens are very good at pack carrying and can carry half their body-weight.

Another use that they are put to is pulling sleighs, and they will do so either singly or as a team of three or five. This is of course a winter occupation but a very useful one. If a person is being carried on a sleigh then a team of five is used. During the spring and summer dogs are not allowed to be loose in the woods or forests in order that the wild life may be undisturbed, so it is only in the winter that the dogs may be loose and enjoy the snow.

In Sweden where it is not so mountainous they do have organised Field Trials and game birds are more plentiful. Goldens in Sweden have overtaken many of their neighbouring countries in popularity and the standard is really high owing to a large number of importations.

Until 1970 Denmark would not allow dogs from Germany or Holland to enter the country unless they spent some time in quarantine. But it was found that the quarantine kennels needed replacing as they were out of date, and the government felt that the cost was not justified as there was no way of preventing wild animals carrying rabies across the border. It was therefore decided to do away with the quarantine restrictions altogether.

However, Denmark's neighbours Norway and Sweden immediately

Checkpoint of Yeo (Charlie), pulling a sleigh in Sweden. Owned by Birgitta and Stefan Jakobsson, Fargelanda, Sweden.

Likely Lad of Yeo with his owner, Mrs Grete-Sofie Mjarum of Norway, who uses him to carry the pack on fishing expeditions.

banned dogs from Denmark from entering their country fearing lest rabies would eventually spread from Europe once the restrictions were lifted by Denmark.

Whereas they were once able to show their dogs internationally this has now ceased in Scandinavia. Dogs from Britain have always been permitted to enter all these countries owing to our stringent quarantine regulations.

In Scandinavia no dog can qualify for the C.I.C.A.B. which is the equivalent of our Challenge Certificate unless he has won a working certificate and in order to become a Champion he must have three C.I.C.A.B.s and at least a second prize in a Field Trial.

Victor carrying pack sacks. He normally carries about forty pounds. Owned by Mrs Agneta Nystrom, Sweden.

A Team of Goldens in Alaska.

I am greatly indebted to Mr and Mrs Totten of the Wyndspelle Kennels Anchorage, Alaska for the following account of their activities with their Goldens. I think it speaks well for the temperament and stamina of the breed.

One must bear in mind that in America their standard does allow an inch more in height and correspondingly more weight. When the ground is fairly even and the snow very dry, which of course it usually is, there is not the resistance when pulling a heavy weight.

However I must point out that in Scandinavia they prefer more lightly-built dogs for pulling sleighs as they do not sink into the snow. Also their pulling harness is somewhat different as shown in the illustrations.

'Enclosed are several pictures of our dogs taken during their first racing season. We didn't set any speed records, but we did beat several husky teams. This year, equipped with more knowledge and a little experience, we hope to get some placements.

We race at the Alaska Sled Dog and Racing Association track in Anchorage, Alaska. The size of the team determines the length of the race. We race three Goldens on a three mile course.

Sled dog training begins in October with the first good snowfall. We train 3-5 miles daily until the official races begin in January. Then we train on alternate days to keep the dogs in condition but not to overtire them before the races. The usual position for the musher is standing on the runners. However on a steep hill or if the dogs are showing signs of over-exertion the musher will run behind the sled.

We run both sexes without any special problems. Not all Goldens are able to run as lead dog. It takes an extremely independent dog with the desire to pull and be out front to be a leader. If you have a dog that has these traits but not strongly enough to be a leader, running him in tandem with a good lead dog will help to develop them.

A typical race day starts with proper foot care. Pads are checked carefully for cracks or signs of wear and tear. The hair protruding beyond the bottom of the pad is carefully clipped level with the pads and vaseline is applied between the pads. This helps to prevent the formation of ice balls. Goldens with tight feet have less problems than those with loose feet. An oil-based solution (some type of grooming oil) sprayed on the leg feathering and pantaloons also helps prevent the build up of ice. The ideal temperature for running is between -20 F and $^{+}$20 F. The dogs do not overheat at these temperatures and have little difficulty with ice. When the temperature is around freezing it is very hard to prevent ice balls and foot care cannot be overstressed.

We use harnesses lined with real lambswool to prevent hair breakage. The bitches can usually wear ready-made harnesses designed for

Opposite: Kanga, Am. Can. Ch. Sun Dance's Tiger Lily Am. C.D.X. Can. C.D. Owned by Mr and Mrs Totten of Anchorage, Alaska. The harness, lined with lambswool, is worn when pulling sleighs.

huskies, but the males generally need custom-made harnesses owing to the greater depth and width of body.

The dogs are then harnessed to the sled, and with one person holding on to the collar of each dog, plus one holding the rear of the sled, we make our way to the start line. The dogs are more than ready to go and have to be physically held back. Each of the dogs has his own special pre-start routine. Strider, lead dog, trembles from nose to tail and moans. Windy, left wheel dog, wags his tail and watches the spectators. Kanga, the right wheel dog, leaps up and down in the air and howls like a husky. The word to go is "Hike" and they are off and running. After mid-November when darkness starts at around 3 pm., the musher wears a head-lamp to light the trail in front of the dogs. Shining the lamp in the appropriate direction helps the dogs to learn "Gee" (right) and "Haw"(left). The "Slow" command is assisted by the use of the brake. Teams start at two-minute intervals; placements are based on the total elapsed time.

During the racing season, their diets are supplemented with extra protein and fat, owing to the extra expenditure of calories in both training and racing. We also feed liver as this is supposed to reduce bruised pads. To prevent dehydration, fresh water is always available, with sometimes a little broth mixed in to encourage drinking.

For practical purposes, this year we used the dogs and sled to go

Kanga, Windy, and Strider harnessed ready for action.

several miles in the woods to get Christmas trees. They did very well hauling trees off trails through a heavy snow.

We have not run our Goldens as a freight team so we do not know what weight they could pull. However, Strider is in training for a weight-pulling competition this winter. We will be in the middle weight class for dogs who weigh between 75 and 125 pounds. The minimum weight for a middle weight qualifying score is 400 pounds to include the weight of the sled. Strider has already proved in training that he can pull this weight from a dead stop. It won't be until this winter's competition that we learn his maximum capacity.

We also use our Goldens for ski-joring (dogs pulling cross-country skiers). We hook up a 30 foot line to the harness of one or more Goldens, depending on how brave you are and how fast you desire to go. Strider routinely pulls my husband (200 pounds plus) for several miles at a time. We have done up to ten miles a day with the dogs doing almost constant pulling.

Our Goldens have readily adapted to the cold climate and cold weather activities usually reserved for the "northern breeds". They are the only all sporting dog team in Alaska, as well as being the only all champion team. We feel that we are really lucky to have such adaptable Goldens, with special pride in our three racing dogs:

Lead dog Strider - Am. Ch. Jabula Thembalisha Am. and Can.CD (Wyndspelle).

R. wheel dog Kanga - Am. Can.Ch. Sun Dance's Tiger Lily Can.CD, Am.CDX (Wyndspelle).

L.wheel dog Windy - Am. Can.Ch. Beckwith's North Wind Am. and Can.CD.(Reddigold).

We feel that these three really prove that "Goldens do it better".'

Dog Shows in Bermuda

The Bermuda Kennel Club hold their series of International Dog Shows annually. In this lovely tropical island about three hundred dogs assemble for a week in which four separate dog shows are held. About two hundred of those taking part are flown into the island by specially chartered planes from America and Canada. These constitute some of the top dogs of these countries. As the show week is held in November at the end of the tourist season the hotels are pleased to offer special rates to exhibitors but even so I am afraid that they would frighten English exhibitors away even if they were able to enter.

The dogs share the luxury living of the best hotels. Most of these have guest chalets or cottages in the grounds which are ideal to live in with the dogs. They consist of a bedroom, bathroom and kitchenette. All the dogs

travel in wire cages and live in these when not being exercised or under supervision.

The shows are held in the Botanical Gardens in Hamilton and the dogs have to be transported by taxi to and fro each day at a staggering charge per mile. The dogs are not benched but remain with their owners, either in their cages or tied to a fence or tree during the show. On entry into the island all dogs have to have their nose prints taken. The three or four judges who are engaged for the shows are changed around for each show so that each breed gets a different judge for each successive show and often the results are quite different.

I had the pleasure of judging Golden Retrievers on one of these occasions a few years ago. Certainly there were not many there but the standard of the gun dog group was high. Nearly seventy different breeds were represented in the various groups as well as Obedience Trials which were run each day with different tests. Several Golden Retrievers were taking part. There are special prizes offered for the local dogs and more and more are being bred on the island.

The whole week is organised by the Bermuda Kennel Club to entertain its visitors. There are sightseeing trips, cocktail parties, boat excursions and on the last night a glittering banquet held at the Princess Hotel. True to British tradition long dresses and black ties are worn. Bermudians are proud to be the oldest British colony and such customs as four o'clock teatime are still adhered to. The beer is very expensive and the drinking water is unreliable as all the water on the island is rainwater which has been drained off the roof of each house and stored in a tank for household use.

Goldens in the Argentine

As far as I can ascertain there have been five Golden Retrievers imported into the Argentine. Two bitches were imported by Mrs D.B.G. Keene and a dog called Parus Major is owned by Colin Graham who is the Principal of St George's College, Quilmes, B.A. In 1965 Mr Charles Blew of Cordoba bought an unrelated dog and bitch from me and took them back with him on the boat. Topic and Topaz of Yeo caused quite a lot of interest as can be imagined. These two are the only ones to have been registered with the Argentine Kennel Club and they have been successfully shown and obtained the title of 'Grand Champion'. Topaz has since produced a litter of seven puppies. Two of these were bought by the Cordoba police and used as trackers. Two went to hunters in the Province of Santa Fé and one bitch went to Colin Graham as a mate for his dog. Mr Blew kept a very promising young dog called Billy Boy of Otten Belchamp which has been shown under English judges, Mr Joe Bradden and Mr Arthur Westlake, and Mr R.M. James. Under each he won the

C.A.C., (Candidate for Champion), three of which are necessary for the title of Champion before going on to the Grand Champion stage which requires five C.G.C. Certificates. He has since won four of these and has been adjudged Best Argentine Bred Dog in a field of fourteen other breeds. This was quite a feather in the cap for Goldens. Mr Blew's dogs are primarily used for retrieving partridge and montaraza as well as other game. But they have other talents for Mr Blew says that he has some twenty kilos of golf balls which the dogs have brought home from a nearby golf course.

Goldens in Canada and America

Golden Retrievers in Canada and the United States are closely linked. The standard is the same and the main difference between them is that in Canada only ten points are required instead of fifteen to become a champion.

The Golden Retriever was recognised as a breed by the Canadian Kennel Club in 1927. It is, however, evident that the first member of the breed to arrive on the American continent was taken there by the Hon. Archie Marjoribanks in 1881. He later visited his sister whose husband was Governor General of Canada and took his Golden Retriever Lady with him. Nothing is known of the progeny she may have had in America or Canada.

It was not until 1928 that Mr B.M. Armstrong of Winnipeg took a real interest in the breed. He later corresponded with Mrs Charlesworth and finally obtained the standard of the breed from her. He died about 1932 and it was then that Col. Magoffin transferred Mr Armstrong's kennel name of 'Gilnockie' to his own estate. He had already established his Rockhaven Kennels in North Vancouver so the name was transferred to his kennel in Denver, Colorado, U.S.A. and it was there that he bred the Gilnockie Golden Retrievers. So it was that Mr Magoffin promoted the breed in Canada as well as in the States. Until that time there were very few indeed. In 1932 the breed was recognised by the American Kennel Club and the English standard adopted, but in 1958 the Golden Retriever Club of America decided to abandon this standard and formulate one of their own.

Mr Christopher Burton who is British by birth played a large part in influencing his great friend Mr Magoffin in breeding Golden Retrievers. I am greatly indebted to him for the information which he has given me and also for his kindness in showing me some parts of Vancouver and introducing me to Mr and Mrs Reid whose kennels we visited and whose hospitality we enjoyed. Mr Burton tells the story of how he and his friend were talking one day of shooting and gun dogs and he asked him which breed he preferred. Having seen Golden Retrievers shot over in England at his brother-in-law's home, Mr Burton suggested a Golden Retriever. Mr Magoffin immediately got up, walked to his study, came back with a cable form, and asked him to send it to his brother-in-law for a young male. The reply came back that such a dog with a Field Trial and show award was obtainable. As a result Speedwell Pluto was sent to Col. Magoffin and was destined to become one of the greatest sires of the breed on the North American continent. He obtained his Canadian and U.S.A. Show Championship as well as several Best in Show awards.

Soon after the arrival of Speedwell Pluto Col. Magoffin bought two bitches called Saffron Chipmunk and Saffron Penelope. These two were out of Dame Daphne who had been exported from England in whelp to Ch. Haulstone Dan. They were to make history for the Rockhaven kennel and the result was a tremendous interest aroused in the breed which proceeded to increase rapidly. At one time there were ninety-eight Goldens in residence in the Rockhaven Kennel alone.

In 1966 I had the pleasure of visiting a number of kennels, shows and Field Trials in America and Canada. This was a great experience for me and during this time I tried to learn as much as possible from the people to whom I spoke of their methods of breeding, rearing and training.

As a nation we are slow to adopt other people's ideas when they do not conform to our own, but as a rule I found that there was a very good reason for our differences.

Americans take their recreation very seriously and I found that the week-ends were usually given over to some form of enjoyment and relaxation. When I entered the huge show ground where the Westchester show was being held at about 7.30 a.m. on a crisp September Sunday morning I could not help thinking, with judging commencing at 8 a.m. sharp, of the storm of protest there would be here if judging started so early. However, one point in their favour is that there is a time-table for each breed to be judged and this is strictly adhered to. Also dogs do not have to be present all the time and can be removed after their classes have finished. How this would be appreciated in Britain. There is good reason for this as dogs exhibited at one show on a Saturday may be on show five hundred miles or more away the next day. It is quite the usual thing for showgoers to load up their trucks with crate upon crate of dogs and equipment on a Friday evening and go off to shows on Saturday and Sunday, returning very often in the early hours of Monday morning. In many cases it is not possible for the owner or breeder to get away like this if they have a family or other commitments so that it is necessary to get a professional handler to take the dogs to the show for you. In Britain we view this with horror. It is no good having good dogs and not showing them, but to do so in America and Canada it means a lot of travelling and expense. No wonder that this is not undertaken lightly and is taken very much more seriously than we do.

As practically every breed is catered for no matter how small the entries it means more judges and rings, but of course the classification of classes is nothing like as big as we are accustomed to in this country. At the Golden Retriever Club of America National Specialty Show the schedule was as follows:

Regular Classes
Puppy Dogs 6 to 9 months
Puppy Dogs 9 to 12 months
Novice
Bred by Exhibitor
American-bred Dogs
Open Dogs
Winners' Dogs (composed of the first prize winners in each of the preceding six classes)

The same classifications are repeated for bitches.

Non-Regular Classes
Veterans Class
Field Trial Class
Stud Dog Class
Brood Bitch Class
Brace Class
Parade of Champions

When a show in America is described as a Specialty Show, this means that it is in effect what we would call a Breed Show. A National Specialty is one covering the whole of America and is the National Breed Show.

America being such a vast country, the club is divided into regions and the regions are divided into chapters. Each hold their own specialty shows throughout the year and are in effect affiliated to the G.R. Club of America. Each year the venue for the National Specialty moves to a different part of the country in order to give breeders an equal chance of attending.

Entry fees are escalating all the time as they are in this country. The Westminster Show which is held just outside New York immediately after Cruft's in February is the great prestige show. It is seldom that any dog is entered in more than one class as is the case over here.

After the Open Class comes the Winners' Class which consists of the winner in each of the preceding classes who has not been beaten. He receives a purple ribbon and points proportionate to the number of males or females as the case may be present at that show.

A Reserve Winners dog is also chosen in the same way as we award a Reserve Challenge Certificate. This dog receives a purple and white ribbon.

When all the bitch classes have finally been judged the winners dog and winners bitch then compete for Best of Winners. The winner then receives a blue and white ribbon and also extra points if the opposite sex had an entry qualifying for higher points. The best of winners then goes on to compete for Best of Breed by meeting the winners of the non-regular classes and any champions entered in the specials class confined to champions only. The winner receives a purple and gold ribbon.

Best of Opposite Sex is selected from the champions of the opposite sex to the Best of Breed, and the winner's dog or winner's bitch, whichever is the opposite sex to Best of Breed. A red and white ribbon is awarded to Best of Opposite Sex. Finally the Best of Breed goes on to the group judging. The various breeds are divided into six groups Sporting, Hound, Working, Terrier, Toy and Non-Sporting and a blue rosette is given to the winner of each group.

The number of points varies according to the area and allocation by the American Kennel Club which is based on the number of dogs and bitches entered and can be altered from year to year. To become a Champion a dog or bitch must win a total of fifteen points under at least three judges; also it must win a minimum of three points at two different shows under different judges. This prevents dogs competing at shows where the breed is not well represented and winning one or two points at a time. The maximum number of points to be won at any show is five. The scale of points is printed in the catalogue for each show. To give an example, one of the National Specialties for Golden Retrievers had a points rating as follows.

	Dogs	Bitches
1 point	2	2
2 points	5	4
3 points	8	7
4 points	13	10
5 points	17	14

It is the Winners' Class which takes the points towards the title and the Best of Breed who goes on hopefully for Group placement and Best in Show.

Unlike shows in this country, dog shows in America and Canada are big business and except for Breed Societies it is usual for the management of 'All Breed Shows' to be undertaken by a show superintendent, who supplies all the equipment and makes all the arrangements, including the printing and mailing of the 'premium lists', which correspond to our 'schedules'.

It is very seldom that there are any cash prizes given but elaborate silver plate in the form of ornaments and dishes of every kind are given to the winners for permanent keeping. Some breeders have a trophy room in their house which is entirely given over to the display of the trophies and ribands won by their dogs. As one can imagine the regular show-goer accumulates an enormous quantity of these trophies.

Out of the substantial entry fee the superintendent takes at least two thirds and as there are literally hundreds of A.K.C. Championship shows yearly a good superintendent may handle as many as thirty to seventy shows a year or even more. This is business in a big way and a show superintendent is a powerful man in the show-going world.

Judges also earn big fees, but to become judges they have to prove their ability by passing certain examinations before they can be licensed by the American Kennel Club. Only licensed judges are elected to judge at recognised shows. Fun matches as they are called are the exception. These correspond to our sanction shows, and are sometimes run by breed societies. Clubs have very little say in the selection of their judges for their big shows which is a pity. Few judges have a real knowledge of the breed standard and I got the impression that breeders were breeding to please the judges rather than stick to the Standard and in consequence the Standard is not being uniformly maintained over the widely separated areas of the country, and the true breed characteristics are being lost. Until more breeders become judges this situation will not improve.

It is a great pity to my mind that the Standard of the breed recognised by the American Golden Retriever Club does not now conform to the British one. No doubt there are reasons for the variation, but Golden Retrievers are in every way British and a British breed they should remain.

One of the basic differences is in size. American Golden dogs vary from 23-24 inches in height and 65-75 pounds in weight. The bitches range from 21½ to 22½ inches in height and 60-70 pounds in weight. The Golden Retriever Club standard in this country is dogs 65-70 pounds and height 22-24 inches. Bitches 55-60 pounds and height 20-22 inches. It will be seen that the overall picture of an American Golden is of a dog who is considerably bigger and certainly weighs more. A great number of Goldens in this country would be too small by American standards. Bitches in particular need to be an inch and a half bigger than our lowest limit to compete in America. Colour on the whole is dark but may be lustrous gold of various shades.

There are so many aspects to the business of making money in the dog world of America; not only show promoters but professional handlers as well. They are very highly paid and often handle as many as twenty to forty dogs at each show. Their charges for handling are considerable, plus an added charge for boarding. If the handler wins a group an additional charge is made and a further charge should the dog win Best in Show. From this it can be seen that dog showing is an expensive hobby, and only a really good dog would be worthy of such an expenditure.

There are also people who trim and groom dogs at the show ready for the ring, and beauty parlours with everything imaginable from jewelled collars to padded coffins for the pets of wealthy owners. Photographers spring up like mushrooms with flash lights, and movie cameras are whirring from every angle of the ringside. But the saddest part for me was to see dogs put into wire cages and heaved into trucks one on top of another for the journey home or on to the next show hundreds of miles away. I never could get used to this and shed many a private tear, particularly when I saw some of my own dogs treated in this way. Their owners say that it is for their own safety whilst travelling but if there is an accident in Britain one seldom hears of a dog being killed. At least they have a chance of jumping to safety but in cages they are trapped and in the case of a car catching fire there is no escape.

I think the real reason is that from the start dogs are generally kept separately in kennels and runs and hardly ever allowed to meet. Consequently to avoid fighting they are caged when travelling. This to me is the worst part of dog breeding in America. They are extremely proud of their kennels which would be good but for the fact that each dog is kennelled separately. Why I cannot imagine. In most instances each dog has a narrow run 8-10 feet long and in this he may spend the whole of his life. In the kennels which I visited there was no regular system of exercising. Possibly at week-ends or in the summer some dogs may be taken out. One person told me that her dogs never went out from autumn until spring, largely on account of the very cold dark winter. In a few instances the kennels were heated but in most cases they were not. One trembles to think what hardships less hardy breeds may have to endure in sub-zero temperatures.

At two establishments which I visited I saw more than a hundred single kennels with Labradors and Golden Retrievers in them. Although they were always scrupulously clean and the dogs looked well fed I felt that everything was very impersonal. It must be understood that of course I am generalising as there are many who keep Goldens as pets or house dogs, and as I have mentioned the climate plays a great part in affecting the circumstances in which they live.

Dogs can suffer as much from heat as from cold and the problem of keeping dogs cool in the hot weather is a very real one. I was pleased to see some kennels where the dogs were kept in the shade of trees. I visited one show in California at the end of October when the temperature was 95 degrees. In such a temperature anything which affords shade is most welcome, and marquees were erected for this purpose, not as we should expect, to keep the rain off. But all too often dogs expire from heat exhaustion. One top winning Golden died in this way on a show circuit whilst I was on tour. Some people have special air conditioning installed in their vehicles in order that the dogs shall not suffer in this way.

One of the biggest snags as I see it is that very few houses have fenced-in gardens, so that house dogs cannot be let out un-accompanied. In that event they would quickly be picked up by 'dog catchers' and thieves who immediately sell them to hospitals for vivisection. There is an enormous trade in stolen dogs for this purpose and I heard many stories of dogs disappearing, taken from kennels and gardens. One person told me her English Setter was lassoed from its exercising run, but the thief was fortunately caught in the act. This sort of thing goes on in the bigger cities, but not so much in the rural areas. However, for this reason it is understandable that dogs do not get the freedom they enjoy in Britain.

Most people have their dogs tattooed on the inside of the ear so that if a dog arrives at a laboratory with a tattoo mark they know that it has probably been stolen and enquiries are made.

American and Canadian Field Trials

I was fortunate in being able to watch the Golden Retriever Club Field Trials, which were held the day before the show, and also the National Field Trials which correspond to our Retriever Championship Trial. This was held about a month later in Canada near Edmonton. It is the practice in America to use live birds either with their legs tied or wings pinioned, but in Canada this is not allowed and only dead birds are used at trials. These trials are run on much the same lines as a cold game test or working test in this country. Everything is arranged so that each dog gets exactly the same retrieve and at the National Field Trial they even went to the extent of moving to fresh ground and measuring the distance to ensure that each dog had an equal chance. As so much duck shooting is done in the northern states and in Canada much store is put on the dog's ability to perform in water. Its water entry must be spectacular and the whole operation fast and controlled. The land tests were all on open ground and were less impressive. They did not compare with open test retrieves in this country.

The water test was held around a stretch of land-locked water of very irregular shape on which floated a number of decoy ducks. Each dog was taken to the water's edge whilst a gun was fired and a live duck thrown to a certain prearranged position. In most cases the duck was returned to its owner in a gasping half dead condition and thrown on a bank in a heap with many others. Some unfortunate ones when thrown came down on hard ground instead of water and were either killed by the impact or stunned. I was so appalled by this heaving mass of gasping shackled ducks, that I made some enquiries and was told that those who survived would be used again. To me this was quite sickening and spoilt what could have been a very pleasant day. My heart was saddened at the thought of this wonderful country with so much to offer the world in wealth, beauty and natural resources and yet whose people could regard life so lightly.

This toughness and inhumanity may be a legacy from the old days when hunting was a matter of survival. Even today when October comes there is a general exodus of men folk who reach for their guns and go off in parties duck hunting in Canada and the northern states. This is followed by pheasant shooting, deer hunting and lastly bear and moose hunting. By Christmas the 'freezer' is well filled and such is the custom of stocking up for the winter that in some towns in the States where game is plentiful there are communal ice boxes where a small fee is paid to rent a deep freeze locker for larger game such as bear and moose. The animal is cut up into joints and stored until it is required.

At each Field Trial meeting there are several different stakes run with a series of different tests. The meeting lasts two or three days and is usually made up of the following stakes. Derby which is similar to our Puppy or Novice Stake, Qualifying Stake, Amateur All-Age Stake and Open All-Age Stake. The number of entries for each stake varies from ten to fifty. At the National Championship Stake which I saw there were over fifty entries and as each dog does exactly the same retrieve it becomes rather tiring to watch. At this particular stake however, the spectators sat inside their transport in a long line like an army of tanks and we moved forward about twenty yards after each dog had performed. It was fortunate that there was no shortage of ground.

Field Trials are organised throughout the whole summer and autumn depending largely on the district. The tests are arranged by the judges and take the form of marked and blind retrieves either single, double and sometimes treble. At all the trials I saw the land work took place on open ground and there was no retrieving from cover such as we have in this country at trials. The dog is expected to take a straight line to the fall and must not work outside the area of the fall which is relatively small. All the dogs are kept on the lead until called into the line. When the first dog has finished his retrieve he is then asked to do what is

termed 'honour' the next dog. This is a test of steadiness and he sits beside his handler off the lead whilst the following dog does his retrieve.

I was quite amazed at the variety of trucks, trailers, caravans, trailer-houses, call them what you will. They came in every shape, size and colour to the scene of the Field Trial. Many are specially constructed trailers with individual kennels usually owned by professional trainers and able to accommodate six to eight dogs. Other caravans or Dormobiles had kennels incorporated inside, one on top of the other with wire doors in front. No expense spared, and the owners wearing the latest sporting fashions with large insignia of the various clubs to which they belonged sewn to their backs, chest and arms. Their head gear was equally bedecked with club badges and quills. A truly colourful scene which I enjoyed immensely.

Ronackers Flashy Figaro making an excellent water entry with powerful drive from the hindquarters. Owned by Mrs Dixie Ackers, California.

I was fortunate in being invited to spend a day with a professional trainer who had a very large kennel by our standards. There were at least a hundred and fifty dogs not all in training as some were boarders but all kept in separate narrow runs with kennels attached. The kennels were not more than four foot square and about three foot six inches high with a hinged lid forming the roof. The entrance for the dog was small and had a rubber flap as previously described in a preceding chapter. They appeared to be made of concrete blocks. In winter they are filled with bracken and with a thick layer of snow on the roof the dogs keep quite warm and comfortable.

The training session took place beside a lake on which there were literally thousands of ducks. None of them made any attempt to take to the air and I gathered that they were so well fed that it was almost impossible for them to do so.

Around the lake there were dense bushes and I was told that it was a favourite place for bear to come at night and feed on the bilberries, and on inspection one could see how the bushes had been stripped. I was rather hopeful that one might appear whilst I was there but I was not lucky. However, during the night I was awakened by heavy snorting outside my window and in the morning I mentioned that I had heard what I thought was a horse wandering around and was told that it was a moose who had paid them a visit during the night.

Not far from the lakeside there was a wooden tower rather like a forest lookout. I discovered that people who wanted to improve their shooting came along and paid a few dollars for ducks to be thrown from the top so that they could practise shooting them. One would have thought that clay pigeons would have served the same purpose. This explained the reason for breeding so many ducks apart from those sold to Field Trial promoters.

Training dogs is done with much more harshness than over here. The dogs do not look at all steady, and in fact are preferred if they look as if they are going to take off at any moment. All sorts of gadgets are used by some trainers, from spiked collars to remote control earphones and electric whips which are used to stop the dogs from running in. One can well understand that Goldens have to be pretty tough if they are going to stand up to this sort of treatment. Unlike Labradors a Golden Retriever does not take well to harsh words, and for this reason they are not so popular among the professionals.

Whilst in California I was invited to a training picnic arranged by the Golden Retriever Club Chapter responsible for that particular area. The morning was spent in training puppies, and in the afternoon I was asked to judge all dogs. These were divided into sexes and different age groups.

The training session was concentrated on retrieving live pigeons, which surprised me and in fact seemed very unwise. The birds had their wings tied with a rubber band and they were thrown into the air to be retrieved by each dog in turn. Many returned dead, and those who had survived several retrieves were thrown again until they expired. I must confess that on seeing one little black and white bird who had survived several retrieves looking at me with its eyes still bright I picked it up unobserved and popped it into the back of an open truck. I have often wondered if it lived and what the surprised owners of the truck thought when they found it.

Obedience Trials

Obedience trials are extremely popular with Golden Retriever owners in America. The more titles which can be added to the dog's name the more they are honoured, and competition is very keen. An event of this kind was held in conjunction with the Golden Retriever National Specialty. There are four obedience titles and in order of rank they are C.D. (Companion Dog) C.D.X. (Companion Dog Excellent) U.D. (Utility Dog) and U.D.T. (Utility Dog Tracker).

Regardless of the dog's placing a dog's score can give him marks towards his Obedience Title. Each set of exercises carries a maximum possible score of two hundred points, but a hundred and seventy is regarded as a passing score. After three of these passing scores gained under three different judges a dog will receive his degree.

Most Golden owners whether successful at shows or not find time to attend Obedience Classes and try to get at least a C.D. title for their dog. I must say that I was impressed by the very slick performance which I saw and in the absence of actual gun dog training classes and tests it does give the dog the chance to prove its ability and retain a sound temperament in the breed.

Tracking
This competition was also organised by the American Golden Retriever Club and I found it extremely interesting to watch. The trail was laid early in the morning about three hours before the competition took place. The dogs taking part wore special harness with a long leash attached at the back near the dog's shoulders. Having been given the scent the dog set off at a good fast walk with nose to ground all the time. The trail was purposely diverted several times to confuse the dog and ended with the dog picking up a small article. In this case it was a glove. It was noticeable that some dogs overran their noses and had to double back to pick up the trail whilst others who were slower worked out the line at a steady speed.

Goldens in Australia and New Zealand

Since this book was first published I have had the great pleasure of judging in Western Australia, Southern Australia and Victoria. I have also visited New South Wales and Queensland where I met a lot of Golden Retriever breeders, visited their kennels and attended some shows.

I was invited to judge the Championship Show of the Golden Retriever Club of New Zealand which was held in Auckland, and during my stay in that country I was taken to the Kennel Club in Wellington which was extremely interesting, and was allowed to delve into their records of Golden Retriever imports.

In both countries there is a great deal of keenness amongst breeders to improve the breed and a number of dogs have been imported from Great Britain.

It is difficult to report on conditions in Australia as a whole since each state has its own club and rules, but it is evident that standards are being maintained and some excellent dogs are being bred. Type varies a little from state to state, largely because of the influence of imported dogs and the fact that there has been very little inter-state breeding.

I was very much impressed by the permanent show grounds, particularly those in Adelaide, Sydney and Melbourne, where the Royal Shows are held each year. These show grounds are used most week-ends by different canine societies. The rings are of grass and surrounded by tiered seating. There are also indoor rings and permanent raised benching for the exhibits. One feature which I thought particularly good was the barrier in front of the benches which prevented the public from getting too near to the dogs and prodding, poking, and patting the exhibits.

The shows are organised very professionally and the stewards have to be fully qualified. The dogs are arranged in numerical order in the collecting ring so that there is no delay between classes. The system of judging is a little different from our own, particularly in the groups where the unbeaten puppies from each gun dog breed compete against each other. This system follows through all the different classes to the Best of Breed and eventually Best Gun Dog. In the event of this being a dog, all the Best Bitches from each breed then have to compete against each other. This method prolongs the judging and means that if you have won a class in your breed during the morning you are bound to wait until late afternoon or evening to compete in the groups. Considering the long distances which people have to travel I found this practice rather difficult to understand as much time is spent waiting for the groups to be judged.

Golden Retrievers have become popular and among the imports from Great Britain have been dogs from some of the well-known kennels including Westley, Anbria, Glennessa, Teacon and my own of Yeo. More recently, artificial insemination has been successfully accomplished using imported frozen semen from a British Champion, namely Camrose Cabus Christopher. This is quite a breakthrough and opens up new avenues with the possibility of further imported semen from different sires.

Among those dogs which have had great influence on the breed in New South Wales are Australian Ch. Nicholas of Yeo and Madonna of Yeo by Ch. Camrose Nicholas of Westley and Yana of Yeo. First imported by Mr Hughes in 1965, they both produced many good offspring. Later, Nicholas of Yeo went to live with Mr Bright in Sydney and the two became devoted companions. Together, in the streets of Sydney, they collected £35,000 for charity. Most of this money was donated to the Dalwood Children's Home, where Nicholas was finally laid to rest at twelve and a half years of age.

In New Zealand the shows are run on more or less the same lines as those in Australia. I judged at a Golden Retriever Club Championship Show which was held in Auckland and thought the standard slightly higher and the dogs more British in type. I think that an additional reason for the variation in type in Australia is that people are encouraged to become judges of breeds other than their own. Aspiring judges can attend

Australian Ch. Tristar of Yeo. By Sh. Ch. Concord of Yeo ex Sweet Klarin (by Int. Ch. Mandingo Buidhe Colum). Owned by Mr Joe Whittal, South Australia.

Australian Ch. Golden Nicholas of Yeo C.D.

a number of classes at the end of which a written examination has to be passed. Whilst this system has its advantages it is easy to see that knowledge is gained in theory but not in practice. I am a firm believer that one has to breed dogs or at least own a particular breed of dog for a long time before one can grasp the finer points. Judges of all varieties do so on basic standards, soundness being of first importance, but many points of breed type may not be recognised by the judge who has not had practical experience of that particular breed.

Although Retriever Trials are held in some parts in Australia there is considerable risk of snake bite to dogs and owners. I discussed this with one lady who told me that although she was keen to preserve the working instinct in the breed she had lost three lovely bitches from snake bite whilst working them; broken hearted, she had decided that it was not worth the risk. When Field Trials are held it is required that anti-snake-bite serum is provided by the society holding the Trials.

In country districts, long grass might appear ideal for training dogs, but this is where deadly snakes are likely to lurk. It is essential to keep short any herbage which may be near the kennels so that it is less likely to harbour snakes. Of course, in the winter there is very little risk as snakes

The Giant Catapult used for throwing birds in trials and training in Western Australia.

Left: The handler has to shoot the birds which his dog retrieves.

Below Left: Rookwood Skylark returning with game.

Below Right: A good delivery to Mr Malcolm Hanford, owner and trainer of the Rookwood Golden Retrievers.

hibernate, but even so they can do this in unlikely places and are not pleased to be disturbed.

One of the nicest things about New Zealand is that there are no snakes, so the beautiful countryside can be enjoyed without any fear. Dogs can be used safely for hunting pheasants and duck, and deer also abound in the natural habitat. The Northern Island is more volcanic and has deep ravines where giant ferns and sub-tropical trees provide excellent cover, so the sportsmen there need dogs which can flush out the birds.

There have been several important imports into New Zealand in recent years. Glennessa Fiddlededee was tragically killed in a road accident but not before he had sired several litters leaving behind some good sound stock. Sh.Ch.Stolford Happy Chance joined Mrs Evans' Vanrose kennels and has sired several litters to date. When Mrs Evans left this country some years ago she took with her a team of good Golden Retrievers which did much to popularise the breed, particularly in the North Island. In the South Island there were already a few dedicated breeders, such as Mrs Hill-Smith and Mrs Joyce Tucker who founded their kennels on a Camrose import. Recently, Mrs Hill-Smith imported a young dog from my kennel and also, Mrs Stonex of Auckland imported a young bitch of my breeding so that there are a number of fresh lines in the breed to work on.

There is much interest in dog breeding in New Zealand and frequent shows are held with classes for most breeds. Although there are many New Zealand judges, judges from other countries, mainly Great Britain, Australia and America, are frequently invited to officiate.

Dog owners have to abide by very strict rules because of the sheep farming and meat production which are the country's most important industries. Every dog has to be licensed and, as a rule, only two dogs are allowed to be kept by any city householder. City dogs have to be dosed for sheep measles every six months by a council official, whilst in rural areas this has to be done every six weeks. This is greatly resented by breeders as the dose given is very potent and can cause the loss of a litter or infertility in both dogs and bitches. Once a year, dogs also have to be dosed for tape worms. This is again done by an official and collecting points are provided where the dogs are chained to railings whilst the dose is administered and takes effect, then samples are taken away and tested. Although it is illegal to give a dog uncooked meat, farm dogs are frequently fed on sheep's carcases and entrails. So important is the meat industry that every precaution is taken, and a stray dog near a sheep farm can be shot on sight. When dogs are imported, regulations are also very strict. Only dogs from rabies-free countries can go directly into New Zealand and even so they have to have a rabies vaccination before admittance and a one month's quarantine on arrival.

As a tailpiece I would like to recount the following story recently sent to me from Mr Hughes of the Goldenheath kennels. He sold a bitch called Goldenheath Jennifer to a friend who, against his advice, took the bitch in his caravan on holiday with the family. On the way a wheel came off the car which made the caravan cartwheel across the road and break in four. None of the family were seriously hurt but they were too shocked to notice that Jennifer had disappeared into the bush.

She was lost at Cobar, which is one of the hottest places in Australia where the temperature is around 100 – 120°F every day and where there is no water for miles.

The alarm was raised and all the newspapers, radio and television stations publicised the news that a dog had been lost in the bush, and that a hundred dollar reward was offered.

About six weeks after the accident a professional trapper saw her. He tried to bait her by putting down kangaroo carcasses in order to keep her alive and entice her to stay in the area. When the owner heard the news that she had been sighted he returned to the district and the professional trapper set fifty rabbit traps which he padded so that if Jennifer was caught her legs would not be too badly hurt.

Her owner accompanied the trapper on his patrol of the traps and at last they heard her cry out, and raced to the spot to release her. The trapper warned the owner that she might bite him but when he called her name and bent down to her she licked his hand.

What a happy reunion this must have been. Although very thin at the time she soon made a complete recovery, and the trapper was more than delighted with his reward as he had twelve children at home.

Index